Heaven wa[illegible] with the m[illegible]

Luke urged Cindy [illegible] them fully clothed. The water streamed over them as she arched back. He nuzzled her neck, his hands seeking her breasts. "Just what I always wanted," he murmured. "My own private wet T-shirt contest."

Cindy opened her eyes to find him looking at her—appreciatively. "There's something to be said for wet denim, too," she replied, loving how his jeans hugged his pelvis and thighs.

Luke laughed. "There's also something to be said for taking a shower the normal way."

Her smile was saucy. "Alone?"

He reached for the hem of her T-shirt. "Nope—naked."

If anyone told **Lorena McCourtney** to go fly a kite, she'd probably say, "I'd love to"—ever since she learned that kites aren't just child's play. During one of her trips to the Oregon coast from her home inland, she was fascinated to see stunt kites in action. So much so that her third Temptation follows her hero and heroine as they, too, race with the wind.

Lorena is both a talented and productive author, having written literally hundreds of short stories before launching her career in romance fiction. She also writes under the pen names Jocelyn Day and Lisa McConnell.

Books by Lorena McCourtney

HARLEQUIN TEMPTATION

73–NO STRINGS ATTACHED
120–BY INVITATION ONLY

With Flying Colors

LORENA McCOURTNEY

Harlequin Books

TORONTO • NEW YORK • LONDON
AMSTERDAM • PARIS • SYDNEY • HAMBURG
STOCKHOLM • ATHENS • TOKYO • MILAN

Published June 1987

ISBN 0-373-25258-7

Printed in Canada

1

THE WIND HAD DIED DOWN, and a silvery ladder of moonlight glimmered on the gently rippling sea. The sounds of sea lions gathered on the offshore rocks drifted across the water, the rough roars punctuated by the sharper barks of seals. The surf whispered sweet nothings against the sand and flirted with Luke Townsend's bare feet.

He dodged the lower edge of a rock that was exposed only at low tide, grimacing a little as his hand encountered an unfamiliar tangle of mussels in the mat of fibrous beard that clung to the rock. The slippery shells, still wet from the retreating tide, gleamed blue-black in the moonlight.

Luke stopped short as he rounded the sharp ridge of rock. Damn. There was someone on the beach, after all, even at this late hour. He started to turn back, but an unexpected movement from the figure standing on the damp sand stopped him.

It was a woman. She raised her hands over her head, arms crossed at the wrists, palms outward. She held the stance for a long moment, head tilted back, hair a sleek sheen of silver. He knew her eyes were closed, even though he was too far away to make out that detail in the moonlight.

What the hell was she doing? He was annoyed that his planned solitary walk had been interrupted. Who was she? Some weirdo out worshipping the moon? An inland visitor performing some crazy tourist rite upon reaching the sea?

Whoever she was, he had no desire to encounter her. Or anyone else.

Again he started to retreat, and again he stopped, unwillingly drawn by the fluid grace of her movements.

Slowly, with infinite elegance, she raised one leg and arched her body backward, head and shoulders following the flowing curve of her arms. Farther and farther she arched, until her fingertips touched the sand. Her legs followed in a graceful arc, as if she were casually walking across the sky, until she was upright again. She rose on her toes with arms spread, balanced for a moment, and then, bending like a supple willow, reversed the movement.

Luke wanted to leave, yet he was stalled by a reluctant curiosity even stronger than the desire to escape before she saw him. She repeated the fluid motions as if her very bones could bend.

Suddenly, with an impatient gesture that contrasted with the elegant grace of her earlier movements, she fumbled with something at her waist and, with a shimmy of her hips, wriggled out of the dark pants she was wearing. She tossed them aside, and her long legs flashed in the moonlight. With a sense of shock, Luke realized that the shapeless sweatshirt was coming next.

He knew he should leave. He had no right to spy on a beautiful sea nymph undressing on a moon-washed beach. Yet he stood spellbound, no longer able to withdraw. He stepped back, trying to conceal himself behind the ragged slant of rock, glad he'd worn dark clothing that made his own body blend into the shadows.

When she tossed the sweatshirt aside, it was with a small sense of relief . . . and guilty disappointment . . . that Luke realized she wasn't naked beneath the outer clothing. A form-fitting dark leotard clung to each curve and flare of her body. She was slim-waisted, but there was an alluring bloom to her hips and breasts. Flat abdomen, taut derriere, regal posture. The leotard was cut high on her legs, emphasizing their slim length and clean lines. Her shining hair, he could see now, was a coil or braid at the back of her head, defining a classic profile.

She stood with hands on hips, legs spread. Her back was to him, the deep scoop of the leotard dipping to reveal shapely shoulder blades and a ripple of spine.

Suddenly she exploded into action. She raced down the beach and did a series of flips, arms and legs and body whirling in a wild surge of power and grace. At the far end, she turned and made another run with a dizzying series of different twists and flips and cartwheels. She seemed not to touch the sand, seemed instead to fly over it as if the laws of gravity had been suspended for her and she might at any moment soar into the night sky.

She slowed to a spinning dance and then a swaying, coquettish walk. Sinking to the sand, she rolled to a handstand, holding it for what seemed an impossible length of time before scissoring her legs to a horizontal line, raising them and then arching to her feet. She made two more runs of powerhouse flips and twists before finally coming to rest on the sand on one knee, head bowed, arms stretched out before her.

My God, she was good! An athlete, an artist . . . a butterfly! Luke wanted to applaud, to cheer. He started to step out from the concealing shadow of the rock, compelled to say something about her extraordinary performance.

Then, she stood up, she shot an alert, self-conscious glance toward the beach trail, as if afraid someone might have seen her. She stood there poised like a wild animal about to run, then hastily retrieved her clothing. It occurred to Luke that he might not have been the only one who had wanted to be alone. If this woman hadn't been avoiding onlookers, she wouldn't have chosen this deserted beach at this moonlit hour.

Peering out from behind the rock, he watched her dress. She didn't turn into a pumpkin in the shapeless sweatshirt and loose pants; she was still graceful and lovely. But it was almost as if the clothing was a disguise, something to conceal any hint of the incredible display of grace and strength he had just seen.

He still wanted to step out and talk to her. The realization shocked him. It had been a long time since he'd really *wanted* to make contact with anyone.

Yet he couldn't do it. He knew he had watched something that wasn't meant to be public, wasn't meant to be seen by curious eyes.

Carefully Luke backtracked around the rock. The tide had turned, and now surf licked his ankles and pant legs. Once his jacket snagged, and he winced at the jerk on tender muscles.

He walked perhaps a half mile up the beach, swinging his arms occasionally to help loosen those sore muscles. Back when he'd jogged five miles a day around the park in Boston, he had smugly thought he was rock hard. He knew better now. Now that he had a job that was more physically demanding than anything he'd ever known, he ached in places he had never realized existed.

And there had been a spell, he reflected bitterly, when he'd been too numb emotionally to know or care whether his body was in working order.

He walked fifty yards or so beyond the distance he'd gone the previous evening, realizing his body was a little less stiff than it had been. Maybe someday his muscles would actually be as hard as he'd once thought they were, he mused wryly.

The woman was gone by the time he made his way back to the rock. He could almost think she'd never been there, except for the maze of footprints rapidly disappearing under the incoming tide. He knelt to touch one of the prints, tracing the defined edges with his fingertips. The sand was cold and damp and impersonal, yielding no impression of the flashing fluidity and energy that had left the imprint . . . and he felt an unexpected sensation of loss. He wondered why she had come to a deserted beach to perform an aerial ballet with only the moon for an audience, why she had wanted to be alone. And was she as lonely as he was?

The realization that he was lonely hit him with full force, like a cold wave that had sneaked up and washed over him. He had thought he was immune to loneliness. He thought he'd convinced himself he didn't need anyone. He had, in fact, determinedly cut himself off from as much of the human race as possible. And yet . . .

Luke pushed back his sleeve, and the faintly glowing numbers on his digital watch told him it was time to leave. Time to return to his empty apartment, pack a lunch and get to work at the lumber mill. He quashed a sigh.

CINDY O'ROURKE WHIPPED her little red Toyota pickup out of the supermarket parking lot. The seemingly inevitable morning fog was already dissipating and a brisk breeze rising. Great! When Cindy had first come to this small town on the Oregon coast, the wind had nearly driven her to distraction, but she took a different view of it now. The brisker the wind, the better for business!

A hand-printed cardboard sign tacked to an electric pole caught her eye. She glanced at her watch. She had a half hour before she had to open the store at nine o'clock. And she never could pass up a garage sale!

She turned down an unpaved side street and parked beside a bank of yellow-flowered Scotch broom. The sale was doing a brisk business. A pleased-looking lady was carting off a floor lamp and a blender.

Cindy wandered among the household goods spread haphazardly over the lawn, considering and regretfully rejecting a desk that was too large for her small cottage. She pawed through a box of magazines, selected two and paid a quarter for them. Then she spotted it.

Her old bed, bought at a previous garage sale when her funds were even more meager than now, was definitely on its last legs. And here was a French Provincial style single bed in white with delicate gold trim; it would fit right in with her decorating scheme in the bedroom. The bed wasn't an antique, of course, but it was lovely. She plopped down on the mattress and found it firm and springy.

"How much for the bed?" she called to the gray-haired lady holding the sale.

"Hundred and fifty for the set," the woman called back.

Cindy hadn't noticed the other bed, hidden under stacks of bedding and used clothing. "How much for just one?"

The woman shook her head. "No, I'll sell them only as a set. However, there was a man here just a few minutes ago who was also interested in buying just one bed. Maybe you could get together. . . ." She looked over her scattering of customers. "But I don't see him now. Tall man with dark hair. Nice looking. But not very friendly," she added with a disapproving sniff.

Cindy glanced around, too. "What was he wearing?"

"Oh . . . blue jeans, or something like that, I think," the woman answered with a vague wave of one hand. She bustled off to sell a bathroom scale.

There was a man just leaving the yard, walking out from behind a patio table and umbrella set. He was tall, although "nice looking" hardly did justice to his darkly handsome face. His stride was long and rapid as if he was in a hurry, but Cindy impulsively called to him, anyway.

"Hey, did you want to buy a bed?"

When he turned he looked startled, as if momentarily thinking he recognized her. Then, apparently deciding he didn't, he glanced around to make certain she was speaking to him. "Pardon me?" he said politely.

The woman had said he was unfriendly, and as Cindy walked toward him she half wished she hadn't said anything. He probably didn't appreciate some strange female yelling across the yard to him. Beneath surprisingly lush black lashes, his dark eyes were guarded.

She stopped in front of him. She had to look up a considerable distance even from her nonpetite five foot seven. "I asked if you were the man who was asking about buying a bed a few minutes ago."

"I inquired, yes. But the lady said she would sell the beds only as a set, and I don't need both of them."

"Neither do I. Maybe we could get together and buy the set and each take one."

Two vertical lines creased the space between his heavy brows as he considered her suggestion. He was wearing a light nylon jacket and jeans that looked new, the fabric still a little stiff over his long legs. His heavy black work boots also looked new.

He hesitated so long that Cindy finally said gently, "It isn't as if we'd be setting up housekeeping together."

The guarded expression retreated, and he laughed. The change was a pleasant surprise. Before, his good looks had made him cool and distant, as untouchable as an image on a movie screen. With the flash of his even, white teeth, she suddenly wasn't sorry she'd called out to him. His angular, sculpted face softened. He became real and alive, and she had an urge to actually reach out and touch him.

"No, I guess not," he agreed. His dark eyes gleamed. "Although it's an interesting idea. . . ."

That teasing, slightly suggestive comment also surprised Cindy. It was something she wouldn't have expected from him, considering his unapproachable expression only moments earlier. Perhaps he was just shy.

She revised that speculation when his gaze roamed her body with no hint of self-consciousness . . . and a certain degree of experienced sophistication. No, not shy. But still a little distant, in spite of the change the smile had made in him.

"There are some other people looking at the beds. We'd better hurry if we want them." Cindy started back across the lawn.

"Well, hey. . . I'm not sure if I do." He followed her in spite of his protest. "I don't know how I'd get mine home."

"I'll haul it in my pickup for you," Cindy called over her shoulder.

The other couple was apparently just looking and moved away when Cindy approached. She reexamined the bed she had previously tested. The owner hurried over, eager to promote a sale.

"They're lovely beds," she said. "Well worth the price I'm asking. I see you found the man I was telling you about."

Cindy rubbed her hand over the headboard, making the gesture obvious enough to draw the woman's attention to a minute scratch. "Well, I don't know," she said, as if her interest had sagged. "The bed is scratched. Would you take a hundred dollars for the set?"

"Oh, my, no!" the woman exclaimed. "These belonged to my mother." All this was an accepted part of the choreography of garage sale bargaining, and Cindy waited for the counteroffer. "But I suppose I could come down to a hundred and thirty."

They bargained back and forth, finally getting down to the fine point of pennies and meeting at a price of one hundred twenty-two dollars and fifty cents. Cindy glanced questioningly at the man, and he nodded approval of the deal. They then had to split the purchase price between them, and the woman wouldn't take checks, so they had to come up with the cash, transferring dollars and change back and forth between the three of them.

Cindy thought they were all done, but then the man announced that someone had given him several dollars too much, and they had to recalculate. When the sale was finally completed, he asked the woman for a receipt. It hadn't occurred to Cindy to ask for one, although it was undoubtedly a good idea.

While the woman went to get a receipt book, Cindy's purchasing partner said, "I've never bought anything at a moving sale before." He smiled. "Thanks for showing me how it's done."

"All you have to do is jump in and start bargaining." Cindy supposed it wasn't all that unusual for someone never to have purchased anything at a garage sale, but it certainly put him in a different classification than most of her friends and acquaintances.

"As I mentioned before, I don't have any way to haul the bed home." He motioned toward a car parked across the street, a sleek silver-gray Alfa Romeo that indeed looked more suitable for transporting a shapely model than a bargain bed. Cindy was surprised. Guys around Steller Beach might spend as much on a vehicle as that classy little sports car must have cost, but they were more likely to put the money into a flashy four-wheel drive pickup loaded with chrome and extras.

Cindy pointed to her own less than flashy Toyota, which she had purchased secondhand. "We can haul them in that—" She glanced at her watch. "But I can't do it right now. I have to get to work."

"That's okay. I have to go home and get some sleep. Maybe we can arrange to pick them up later."

"Night worker?"

He nodded. "Pulling green chain at the Blue Heron lumber mill."

"Rough job." In fact, Cindy knew it was the heaviest, hardest labor at the mill. The men who pulled green chain handled the rough lumber immediately after it was sawed off the log, when it was still heavy with moisture. A saying around timber country was that if you weren't a man when you started on the green chain, you would be when you finished. If you survived.

The woman returned with receipt book and pen. She agreed that the beds could stay until evening, although she wouldn't be personally responsible for them. "Now who do I make this receipt out to?"

"Luke Townsend."

"Cindy O'Rourke."

The woman wrote out the receipt, handed it to Luke and then went off to help another customer. He stood there looking at the slip of paper with an undecided expression on his face.

Finally he said, "You can have the receipt, if you like." He held it out to her.

"That's okay. I trust you."

Her answer brought a wry quirk to his mouth, but he didn't say anything. Instead he surprised Cindy by tearing the receipt in two and handing one to her. "There, now each of us knows that only the person with the other half of the receipt is entitled to the other bed. Accept no substitutes." He spoke as solemnly as if they had just entered into a blood-bond conspiracy.

Cindy nodded with the same hint of conspiracy. "Meet you here about six o'clock? Shall we synchronize watches?"

She held out a slim hand and pushed back the sleeve of her blouse. He placed his larger hand beside it, his heavy-boned wrist making hers look fragile.

"Watches synchronized. Six o'clock," he affirmed.

LUKE WENT BACK to his apartment—bedroom, living room, efficiency kitchen—showered, took two aspirins to ease his tired muscles and crawled into the double bed that took up most of the space in the tiny room. He had already eaten breakfast, having come directly home from the mill when he'd got off work at seven a.m. When he had found he was out of aspirin, he'd driven down to the market to buy some. He'd spotted the single bed on his way home and stopped to inquire about it, thinking it would take up less space than the lumpy double that had come with the apartment. Wryly he realized the king-size bed he'd had in his condo back in Boston would have reached almost wall to wall in this cramped room.

The aspirin dulled the pain in his muscles, but he couldn't sleep. Partly that was because he still hadn't adjusted to the reversal of day and night in his life, even though his nights had been restless and sleepless long before the lumber-mill job. But more than that was keeping him awake.

Was Cindy O'Rourke the woman he'd seen on the beach?

He had been watching for her ever since that one-sided meeting four evenings before. He'd been back to the beach, hoping to see her again, but she had never been there. Still, Steller Beach was a small town, and he figured he'd run into her sooner or later—if she hadn't been just a tourist passing through.

When Cindy had first spoken to him at the sale, he'd instantly thought she was the woman he'd been watching for. She had the same color hair, a striking shade of pale blond, and was approximately the same height and build. Just as quickly, however, doubt had replaced the sense of recognition. There were as many differences as similarities between the two. The woman on the beach had worn her hair pulled back from her face in a sleek and classic style. Cindy's loose, tousled blond hair bounced irrepressibly around her neck and shoulders. Both had high cheekbones, but Cindy's pert nose was a bit upturned for a classic profile.

Actually, he realized, he couldn't even be positive about a similarity in hair color. The moonlight had been deceptive, turning even the dark beach rocks to gleaming, ragged mountains of silver.

He tried to compare the probable ages of the two women, but there, too, he couldn't arrive at a decisive answer. The woman on the beach was ageless. She might have been a mature eighteen or a serene thirty-eight. Cindy looked to be somewhere between twenty-two and twenty-seven. There was a maturity about her, yet at the same time a saucy hint of playfulness. She had seemed friendly and sociable, hardly the type of woman to seek a solitary moonlit beach.

He flopped over on his other side. He could just ask Cindy, of course, if she'd been practicing gymnastics on the beach. Yet if she was the woman he'd seen, she might not appreciate his intrusion on her privacy. He didn't want to scare her off, and the mysterious woman on the beach had looked ready to run.

It had been a long time since he'd engaged in the banter he'd enjoyed with Cindy. And her quick, confident, "I trust you," was something he hadn't heard in an equally long time, something that meant more to him than any number of flirtatious words. No, he definitely didn't want to scare her off.

And he was looking forward to six o'clock.

CINDY PUT IN A BUSY DAY at the kite shop where she was manager, an average day except for the fact that she sold one of the four-hundred dollar, limited-edition Delta Dragon kites. It was a spectacular design, two flamboyantly colored dragons battling on the background of a black delta kite with an eight-foot span. The purchaser, from California, had said she had no intention of flying the kite; it was going to decorate the den of her new home. Then, using a bit of gentle salesmanship, Cindy had talked the woman into buying a smaller, inexpensive model so that she could enjoy the carefree fun of actually flying a kite instead of just admiring it on the wall.

Between customers Cindy's thoughts bounced back regularly to Luke Townsend. She kept thinking about the husky appeal of his voice, the appraising measure of his eyes, the taper of his body from solid shoulders to lean hips. The woman at the moving sale had judged him unfriendly, but Cindy optimistically thought serious would be more appropriate. She found his hint of reserve intriguing, far more appealing than calculated charm or egotistical aggressiveness. He had a certain intrinsic sexiness, deeper than a glossy surface appeal. And that rare flash of a smile transformed him.

She was certain he hadn't been pulling green chain at the lumber mill for long. The new work clothes had told her that, but she had also observed a certain stiffness in his back and stride that spoke of muscles sore from unaccustomed, hard physical work. Cindy knew from long experience the stiffness and aches and pains that came from working muscles to their limit—and beyond.

She locked up the kite shop at five-thirty. The clear sky promised a lovely moonlit evening on the beach, but she wasn't tempted to make another solitary excursion there; she had those urges only rarely, although she still did her stretching and flexibility exercises regularly at home.

She had to stop by the twenty-four-hour machine at the bank, and Luke already had the beds dismantled when she arrived. If she interpreted correctly, his smile and wave said he was glad to see her.

"I figured we'd have to take the beds apart to get them in your pickup."

"Good idea." She expertly backed the vehicle into the driveway, getting as close to the twin mattresses as she could without driving on the grass. She hooked her thumbs in her pants' pockets and deliberately swaggered as she strode over to him. "You got half a receipt to show you're entitled to one of these beds, mister?"

He reached into his shirt pocket and fished out the ragged slip of paper. "Where's yours?"

"Actually, I've probably lost it by now," Cindy admitted. "Trust me?"

"Well, I'm not sure." He scrutinized her in exaggerated detail, his gaze sliding over her curves as if mentally measuring them for a bikini. Finally he said, "Okay, I guess you're not an impostor. You're my real bed partner."

Cindy blinked. "Would you...uh...mind rephrasing that?"

"I believe the receipt said, 'Sold to Luke Townsend and Cindy O'Rourke, one set of twin beds.' That makes us bed partners," he pointed out. He laughed at her squirm of discomfort and added, "They look like well-made beds. I think we made a good buy."

He was wearing tan cords now with jogging shoes—one of the high-priced brands, she realized—and the same nylon jacket. He wasn't pale; a dark complexion went naturally with his walnut-brown hair and eyes. But Cindy's skin was tanned much darker than his, dark enough to make her blond hair pale into a sunshiny halo around her face. Everyone thought the Oregon coast drowned in rain all winter, but there were really some very pleasant days. And two weeks with her family in the Arizona sunshine hadn't hurt, either. She tucked a renegade wisp of hair behind one ear.

"Been jogging?" she inquired conversationally.

He hesitated, and she had the odd impression that he carefully weighed every personal question before answering, even so simple a one as this.

"No. I'm just wearing running shoes because they're comfortable." Then, as if to forestall any more questions about his personal activities, he said, "Shall we try to take both beds in one load or make two trips?"

"I think we can haul them both at the same time. I have a confession to make." She smiled appealingly. "I have to move my old bed out before I can get this one in. I was hoping I might persuade you to help me."

"Then I'll confess, too. I'm in the same situation."

She was surprised. "Why are you buying a bed if you already have one?"

"Why are you?" he returned logically.

"My old one is worn out."

He wickedly arched a dark eyebrow, giving a risqué meaning to her guileless words, and Cindy felt herself blushing. "Not what you're thinking," she muttered.

"How do you know what I'm thinking?" he challenged. "One should never jump to conclusions." There was an undercurrent of warning in the words in spite of their lightness.

"Okay, what were you thinking?"

He hesitated and then laughed, erasing that hint of hostility that had momentarily invaded their friendly sparring. "Never mind."

"Mine is simply an old, old bed," she said firmly.

They loaded the dismantled beds into the pickup, leaning the mattresses and box springs against the side of the truck's metal canopy. "Where do we go first?" Cindy asked. "Your place or mine?" Immediately she realized that she'd left herself wide open for another comment, but Luke just smiled and let that opportunity pass. She had the impression that he was a little rusty at teasing.

"My apartment is just a few blocks away," he said. "I'll lead the way in my car."

Cindy followed the sporty convertible to an older house that had been remodeled to make a separate apartment on the second floor. Luke came around to the pickup window.

"Actually, all we need do is unload the bed and leave it here. I can move the old one out and carry this one in later."

"Oh, no. A deal is a deal," she assured him. "I need your help moving my bed, so I'll help move yours."

There was an outside entrance up a flight of weathered stairs. Cindy took a surreptitious glance around the apartment, curious but not wanting to show it.

The living room was clean, the inexpensive furniture neutral, as if it had been chosen with an eye toward not offending anyone. She presumed it had come with the apartment. Except for a copy of *The Wall Street Journal* on the coffee table, there were no personal touches in the room. The newspaper surprised and further puzzled her. It seemed unlikely reading material for a man who pulled green chain at a lumber mill.

The small kitchen was also clean and impersonal. A little reluctantly she followed Luke into the bedroom, suddenly realizing that in accompanying a man she barely knew to his apartment she had put herself in a rather compromising position.

Yet his attention seemed centered on getting the double bed out of the tiny room, which relieved her. He yanked off blankets and sheets. "The landlady said I could put this bed in the garage. I'd have moved it earlier except that I didn't wake up until just a little while ago, and I didn't want to be late meeting you."

"You were afraid I'd make off with both beds?" she kidded.

"No, I just didn't want to miss you—" He broke off, evidently noting rather tardily that she'd been teasing. He smiled self-consciously. "Yeah," he amended in a drawl. "I thought maybe you were a professional bed bandit."

Cindy smiled, too, pleased with his admission that he'd been eager to see her again. Flippantly she said, "Well, you never can tell. I imagine bed bandits come in all shapes and sizes."

He gave her another glance that said he liked the shape of this one.

They wrestled the old bed downstairs and the new one upstairs. The white-and-gold bed looked a little delicate and out of place in the nondescript room, but it didn't take up as much space as the clumsy old double.

"Okay, on to your place." Luke reached into the closet to get a heavier jacket, and the open door revealed a lineup of expensive business suits. They seemed as incongruous as *The Wall Street Journal* had, but Cindy didn't know him well enough to ask for an explanation, of course.

She led the way to her place. Darkness had gathered, and she kept an eye on the headlights in her rearview mirror. She was afraid she might lose Luke on the twists and turns to her secluded cottage, but he stuck right with her.

Luke's glance around her tiny dwelling was openly curious, not surreptitious. She glanced around, too, wondering how it appeared to him. In contrast to the impersonal ambience of his apartment, her cottage reflected both her personality and work.

An oversized collage of kites that she had designed took up most of one living-room wall, the vivid colors brightening the windowless area. An airy mobile that she'd made of driftwood and shells hung in one corner. Green ferns and a spider plant cascaded from a shelf over the glassed-in breakfast nook at one end of the kitchen, which was her only dining area.

Her mother had urged her to bring her awards and trophies back with her when she returned from the Arizona trip, but she had politely declined. Mrs. O'Rourke had never seemed to realize that to Cindy the trophies weren't a reminder of past success. They brought back memories of broken dreams and failure, failure she had learned to live with but that was painful to remember nevertheless.

Luke looked around her feminine bedroom with the same lack of self-consciousness. She'd covered the ugly old cracked-plaster walls with a ceiling-to-floor drapery of delicate woodsy fabric, giving the room the air of a secluded woodland glade. A small but intricately fashioned Japanese box kite of real silk hung in one corner. The bedspread repeated the pale green of the graceful trees in the wall fabric, and there were throw pillows of cream and sunrise pink.

Beneath the ruffled spread, however, was the reality of the old bed, the foot end propped up on wooden blocks because the legs had been broken off before she acquired it, the mattress patched with tape.

Luke laughed when he saw the bedraggled bed in its naked state, the chuckle a deliciously husky sound that added an unfamiliar male spice to the femininity of the room. "You do need a new bed," he agreed.

They repeated the bed-out, bed-in process, leaning the old one against the inside wall of the attached carport. Their small talk was casual. Once they almost collided in the bedroom doorway as they carried parts to and fro. Luke lifted his free hand to steady her, the touch brief and utilitarian, but afterward she felt as if she was wearing an armband of glowing warmth from the imprint of his fingers.

A little later, when he was shoving the parts of the new bed back together, his body suddenly went rigid, and he grabbed the left side of his chest. He said nothing, but a muscle ridged his jaw as he gritted his teeth in pain.

"What is it?" Alarmed, Cindy rushed to his side, her hands instinctively reaching out to him. "What's wrong? Is it your heart?"

2

"NOT UNLESS you've stolen it." Luke managed a strained smile. "I just get these damn muscle cramps once in a while. Kind of like a charley horse, only it's in a chest muscle. Hurts like hell." The words were shallow and jerky, as if it hurt him to breathe.

Without stopping to consider what she was doing, Cindy swiftly unbuttoned his shirt. She started massaging the rigid muscle, but his chest was too high for her to get a good grip.

"Lie down," she commanded. She didn't think about the propriety of telling a near stranger to lie down in her bedroom. She'd had many a painful muscle cramp and knew how much they hurt.

His eyes moved, but he didn't turn his head, the pain locking his neck muscles, too. "Where?" The bed was still a haphazard collection of disconnected pieces.

"On the floor."

He complied, and Cindy went to work with practiced skill on the cramp. She squeezed and kneaded, keeping the pressure firm but not rough. The muscle felt sculptured in marble. "Try to relax your other muscles. Just let everything go limp. Breathe naturally, if you can. How long have you been having cramps like this?"

"Just since I've been working at the mill. I went to a doctor, and they're nothing serious. Just annoying as hell."

"You aren't accustomed to that kind of work?" Teeth gritted against the pain, he didn't respond, and she didn't pursue the subject.

She kept working until he took a deeper breath and said, "It's starting to loosen up."

"I can feel that." The muscle was slowly beginning to relax and soften to normal pliancy, but she kept massaging, working her hands outward beyond the affected area.

"Are you a nurse?" he asked.

"No." She used one hand to brush the hair out of her eyes, the other to keep the massage going.

"You're very good at this." He finally took a full, deep breath, expanding his chest to maximum capacity. "I think it's about back to normal. Thanks."

She felt a light touch at the sides of her waist, and with horrified astonishment suddenly realized that at some point in her ministrations she had straddled his body in order to get a better grip on the cramped muscle. Her knees were on either side of him, her bottom pressed against his abdomen. It felt warm and taut. She started to rise, but his grip tightened, holding her in place.

"Don't," he whispered. "You feel so good next to me."

"I—I think the cramp is all gone."

Yet she made no further effort to rise, made no move at all except to study him with eyes that were very wide and blue. His open shirt revealed the full expanse of his chest. It was the kind of chest and body Cindy had always admired most in a man. Long, smooth muscles, more densely bunched in the area of his nipples. A heavy ridge of collarbone and a wide rib cage tapering to a long, flexible midsection. No rough mat of hair to mar the sleek expanse of skin, just a dark, silky sprinkling of hairs that formed a line of curling whorls around his navel and then disappeared under the vee of her own legs spread so intimately across his body.

His hands moved upward from her waist, sliding beneath the blouse that had come loose from the band of her jeans as she'd concentrated on the massage. She felt thumbs cross her midriff, palms glide over the wavy indentations of her ribs, fingertips explore the long muscles of her back and brush the sides of her breasts.

"So warm and inviting," he whispered. "So soft and . . ."

Her body felt as if it were swelling under his touch, blooming like some exotic flower, and then she realized that the feeling was centered in her breasts. They felt warm and heavy, and it took all her willpower to put down the unexpected rush of desire; she wanted far more than that fleeting brush of fingertips.

"I suppose I'm taking unfair advantage," he whispered.

"I suppose you are." Her eyes wanted to drift shut, and she blinked to keep them open. But she made no move to stop the sensuous magic of his hands gently stroking the bare skin of her back.

"Angry?"

"No. . . ." Just surprised at the depth of her own reaction to his touch, she realized. She straightened her shoulders, and his hands dropped to clasp her hips loosely. She folded her arms against her chest because she had a peculiar desire to let them wander over his lean body.

"Surely with a name like O'Rourke you must have an Irish temper that may explode any moment."

"I'm not Irish. I was born a good old American Jones." Although that didn't mean she was without a temper. At the moment, however, she simply didn't understand herself. She was expert at making tart, amusing comments to ease out of situations that threatened to turn too intimate, but she wasn't doing that now. She was just sitting here on the warm cushion of his body as if it was the most natural arrangement in the world.

"You married an O'Rourke?" he speculated, after considering her answer for a moment. "You're divorced?"

She shook her head, relieved that he apparently intended to talk rather than take advantage of their intimate position. "No, I've never been married. And I'm never going to be divorced," she added as an afterthought.

"Then how did you become an O'Rourke?"

"It really isn't important—"

"I want to know." He brought his legs up behind her and gently guided her body so that her back leaned against his thighs. He shifted beneath her, making himself more comfortable but at the same time sending little shock waves of awareness rippling through her. "Tell me." He rested his hands on her thighs.

"It really isn't a complicated story. I guess it started before I was born, when my mother went to New York City from a little town in Connecticut to be a ballerina. She married a man named Jones, and then I was born. Cinnamon Jones, she named me."

"Cinnamon." Luke rolled the name around on his tongue as if he liked the taste of it.

Cindy momentarily considered the incongruousness of sitting on the abdomen of a man she hardly knew, her back resting against his bent legs, telling him about the circumstances that had changed her from a Jones to an O'Rourke. But somehow the unlikelihood of the situation didn't really seem important, and she continued.

"Then Mr. Jones went away." Cindy never had been able to think of that man, whom she couldn't even remember, as her father. She thought of him as The Invisible Mr. Jones when she thought of him at all. She'd never had the slightest desire to make contact with him. "And my mother and I were alone."

"That must have been very difficult for both of you."

"I really can't remember, but I'm sure it was very hard for her. She was a very talented ballerina. She has a scrapbook of photos and clippings describing what she'd done and what great promise she showed. And then a handsome Irish mining engineer named Mike O'Rourke came to town. They had a whirlwind two-week courtship, after which he carried her—and me—off to Arizona with him."

"Your mother gave up being a ballerina?"

"A little mining town named Sundust, Arizona doesn't offer much in the way of opportunity for a ballerina. Eighteen hundred people, about a hundred miles from nowhere."

"Did she regret giving up her career for love?"

"I don't think so." Cindy's earliest memories were of Mike and her mother clowning and laughing, always kissing and hugging and including her in their embraces. "I have two younger brothers, technically half brothers, of course, although I never think of them that way. And they're both as big and brawny and handsome as their father."

"And so what are you doing here in Oregon all by yourself?"

Suddenly Cindy became vague. "Oh...just enjoying life." She turned the question back to him. "What are *you* doing here?"

"Right now I'm wondering if you'll have dinner with me. You haven't eaten, have you?" His hands tightened lightly on her thighs, sending exquisite quivering little flashes up to her abdomen.

"Shouldn't you be eating breakfast?" Cindy asked. "Isn't this morning if you're a night worker?"

"So far I haven't been able to reverse my life that completely."

"How long have you been working at the mill?"

"A couple of weeks. I tried to get a job in the woods on a big reforestation project the company has going on their logged-over timberland, but there weren't any openings. I'd have preferred working in the woods to being in the mill. But I was lucky to get any job at all. Jobs are scarce."

"I noticed that you have out-of-state license plates. Massachusetts, aren't they?"

"I haven't had time to get Oregon plates yet." She noted a slight narrowing of his dark eyes, and she knew she was treading on shaky ground.

"You don't strike me as a . . . typical mill worker," she ventured, testing her suspicion that if she started asking too many questions he'd change the subject. She was right. He didn't like prying. He deftly ended the questioning right there.

"I must say this is the coziest and most enjoyable discussion I've had in a long time, but I'm getting hungry. Aren't you?"

He made a movement beneath her that urged her to get up but at the same time was accidentally quite sensuous, making her feel as if she was riding a living wave. At least she thought the seductiveness was an accident. She stood up, surprised at her own reluctance to leave his solid body; surprised, too, by the wickedly erotic thoughts that kept darting through her mind. They were so fleeting as to be almost subconscious, but she knew they were there. She hoped he didn't.

THEY FINISHED putting the bed together, then went to the Chowder House, a casual restaurant specializing in local seafood. Cindy knew the waitress. Her daughter had worked part-time for Cindy in the kite shop the previous summer.

Cindy inquired about the girl, who was now in college, and the two women exchanged a few pleasantries. Cindy introduced Luke, mentioning that he was working at the sawmill. He acknowledged the introduction with a polite nod and murmur.

"Your husband works there, too, doesn't he?" Cindy asked. "On day shift?"

Cece Bennett wrinkled her nose. "Jake got promoted to foreman, but he had to go back on nights to do it. Some promotion." She rolled her eyes expressively as she set menus in front of them. "He usually eats in here when I'm working, and that's about all we see of each other these days. I just hope he doesn't catch that miserable flu that's going around the mill."

Cindy turned to Luke. "Perhaps you know Cece's husband, since he's on night shift. Jake Bennett?"

"Probably." The statement wasn't discourteous, but it was cool enough to discourage further probing into mutual acquaintances. Luke picked up the menu and started studying it.

Cindy's temper flared. What was he—some sort of snob who considered himself too good to associate with waitresses and other mill workers? She ordered without looking at the menu, suddenly disappointed in him. She hated snobbery.

"Chowder and the salad bar, please, Cece."

Luke ordered the salmon steak and baked potato. He politely asked for coffee immediately.

Conversation during the meal lagged, the little that was said hopscotching awkwardly around impersonal subjects. Luke asked about the origins of the town's name, Steller Beach, and Cindy told him that it came from the type of sea lions that were numerous in the area. They talked briefly about the depressed fishing industry and a new resort that was being built up the coast. Luke didn't ask any more personal questions, and Cindy suspected that was because he didn't want to be under any obligation to answer some of the same about himself.

Suddenly it occurred to her that perhaps he was married. He wasn't wearing a wedding ring, but many men in rough labor jobs didn't; there was always a possibility of getting a ring hung up on dangerous machinery. Perhaps he'd just come here to get a job and had a wife and kids stashed somewhere.

Once she'd thought of this, she couldn't just let the doubt lie there like a bomb waiting to explode. She didn't bother with tactful preliminaries. "Luke, are you married?"

He looked up, surprise overriding his usual reserve. "Good Lord, no!" The answer was so immediate, so nonevasive that she had no doubt about its truth. "Whatever made you ask that?"

"It just occurred to me."

He hesitated and then said, "I was engaged once, but that's as close as I ever got."

"What happened?"

"We just drifted apart." The reserved wariness was back again, and suddenly Cindy knew his attitude toward the waitress hadn't been snobbery. He'd have reacted the same no matter whom she'd introduced him to. Luke was just wary of people in general. Including herself.

Impulsively she asked, "Luke, do you dislike people?"

"What people?"

She suspected he'd deliberately misunderstood her question. "Any people," she answered impatiently. "People in general."

His answer was slow in coming, as if he was carefully measuring and weighing the words. "I don't dislike them, but I've been disillusioned a few times. I've found it's better not to be too trusting or get too involved."

"That can be a very lonely philosophy to live by."

He nodded soberly. "Yes, it can. But the bottom line is that you really have only yourself to depend on. I believe in self-reliance and self-sufficiency."

"Are you a workaholic?"

"I suppose you could say that. At least I used to be," he amended slightly. "Does it show?"

Cindy smiled. "Just guessing." But what she really wanted to say was, "Loosen up. Enjoy life. There are lots of good people in the world. Nice, wonderful people. Trust them. Get involved. Have some fun with them." There was a certain tension about him that had nothing to do with sore muscles. But she didn't know him well enough, of course, to offer gratuitous advice. It was also obvious that he was a person who lived by his own rules; he wouldn't appreciate advice any more than he did prying.

They drove back to Cindy's cottage through a damp fog that had rolled in with the suddenness typical of the Oregon coast. It was cozy inside the small car, fog blurring and softening the oncoming headlights. Cozy and very intimate.

In her driveway, with one hand on the door, Cindy said quickly, "Thanks for dinner. You needn't walk me to the door. That mist is almost rain."

"I'll walk you to the door. I want to ask you something."

They got out of the car, and uneasily she asked, "Something . . . personal?"

"Very." He brushed aside the branches of a rhododendron bush to keep the wet leaves from touching her.

"About tonight?"

"Yes."

The walkway was made of irregular slabs of flat rock with little ridges of grass between. Cindy nervously stumbled over one clump, and Luke's hand was right there to steady her. Feeling her arm tingle under his touch did nothing to decrease her nervousness. She knew what was coming.

At the doorway he turned her to face him, his hands loosely enclosing her waist. Her hands automatically rose to his shoulders, but she clasped his collar and kept her fingers from slipping around his neck. She had left a lamp on in the cottage, and its glow dimly lit his face. Jewels of moisture glistened in his hair and eyebrows, emphasizing that certain aura of mystery that lingered around him.

"You're very sweet and lovely, Cinnamon O'Rourke." His hands moved gently at her waist, short glides that ventured neither too far up nor down, as if they were on a tightly controlled leash. He smiled. "I take it you're not going to invite me in."

"I don't think it would be a good idea," she agreed.

"What if I ask to come in?"

"Is that the personal question you were planning to ask me?"

"Hmm. Although that isn't all of it."

"I'm sure it isn't!" Her temper flared as it had earlier, and she tried to jerk out of his arms, but they closed around her, locking her body to his. Electricity flashed through her thighs when they met his. She arched backward, realizing that was a mistake when the movement only increased the intimacy of the contact between them.

"Temper, temper," he chided.

"If you tell me that I'm cute when I'm angry, you may have something worse than a muscle cramp," Cindy warned.

"I was merely going to ask if I could talk you into giving my back a good massage. You seem to know what you're doing, and all the bending and lifting at work makes my back feel as if a couple of Paul Bunyan-sized loggers have been jumping up and down on it."

"You want a back massage?" Cindy asked. She tilted her head to look up at him. "That's *all* you want?"

"What did you think I was going to suggest?" He laughed when she didn't answer. Teasingly he added, "You're disappointed with my request?"

"I am n-not disappointed!" she sputtered.

"Then you'll do it?"

Cindy considered for a moment. She was no professional masseuse, but she could give a reasonably proficient rub-down that might help loosen his back muscles and relieve the pain. She knew he wasn't just pretending; she'd already noted the telltale stiffness.

"Just a back massage?" she finally asked cautiously. "Nothing more?"

"Sweet Cinnamon, when you and I make love—"

"Make l-love!" Cindy echoed, choking and sputtering again. "Who said anything about making love?"

He laughed lightly and repeated the words that attacked her heart like a flutter of butterfly wings. "When we make love, we are not going to do it under the constraint of a time limit, when I have to keep one eye on the clock. This is a work night for me, remember? And I still have to go home, pack a lunch and drive out to the mill."

When she still didn't produce the key to the cottage, Luke added, "How about if I give my solemn oath?" He held up one hand, palm toward her. "I, Luke Townsend, do hereby solemnly swear that—"

"Never mind," Cindy muttered. She fished the key out of her purse and opened the door.

Luke followed Cindy into the cottage. She held out a warning hand when he reached the doorway between the kitchen and living room.

"Wait here," she commanded.

Luke stood as instructed, watching as she marched through each room, apparently turning on every light in order to leave no dangerous pockets of darkness. She disappeared into the bedroom and returned a moment later with a roll of foam rubber and a blanket.

Luke had been studying the colorful display on the far wall. He moved across the room and touched the lightweight fabric stretched tautly across a fragile wood and fiberglass frame. "What are these? Kites?"

"Yes." She rolled out the pad and spread the blanket over it. "Take off your shirt and lie down on the mat. Face down."

He followed her instructions, pillowing his cheek on his hands with his eyes toward the kites. He had recognized the objects, but they were like no kites he had ever seen. One was a huge, brilliant red triangle with the silhouettes of two ballerinas in white pirouetting on either side of a central fin of material. Another was a hexagon with appliques of cheerful "happy day" faces. The third was a more conventional diamond shape, but a unicorn pranced across it, and the tail formed a kaleidoscope of colorful streamers. "Do you have a hobby of making or flying kites?" he asked.

"Kites are my living." She disappeared into the bedroom again and returned with a bottle of liquid.

"I'd just as soon not go to work smelling like a rose garden."

"You won't."

She poured a little of the lotion into one hand and rubbed her hands together. Luke caught a pleasingly fresh, slightly minty scent. A moment later her hands were on his shoulders, the lotion already warmed to body temperature. He closed his eyes, letting the soothing touch penetrate skin and muscles. She worked with silent concentration on the densely bunched muscles between his neck and left shoulder, then switched to the right shoulder.

"You're welcome to sit in the middle of my back, if that would be more convenient for you," Luke offered.

He felt no touch at all for a moment, and he lifted his head to look at her. She was sitting back on her heels, apparently considering the suggestion with a certain amount of apprehension. Her blue eyes, he noted, weren't a uniform blue. There was a ring of navy around the outside edge. But the inner area was lighter, dancing with the sparkle of sunlight on blue water even as she regarded him seriously.

"I won't bite," he added gently.

"I don't think a professional masseuse parks herself in the middle of a client's back," she said finally. He suspected a bite was not what worried her.

"Well, whatever works best for you." He turned his face in the opposite direction, as if it didn't matter to him, but he was pleased when a moment later he felt her knees slip around him. She massaged the long muscles on either side of his spine, her body rising and dipping with the long strokes, her bottom making fleeting but rhythmic contact with his buttocks.

"How do you make a living with kites?" He was curious, of course, but the question was as much to divert his own attention from the sensuous pleasure of her body moving over him as to obtain information. He could, he reflected wryly, regret that solemn oath he had made at the door.

"I'm manager of a kite shop over on North Jetty Avenue."

"Just kites, nothing else?"

"Well, kite accessories, too, of course. String and instructional materials and a few little souvenir items. But mostly just kites of all kinds, everything from fifty-foot dragons to fighters and stunt kites. Come over to the shop sometime, and I'll show you."

"There's really that much interest in kites?"

Cindy laughed. "Haven't you noticed the wind here?" She switched to a different movement, with her hands curved around his ribs. Her touch felt good, but she was leaning forward now, and he regretted the loss of that tantalizing bounce of her firm bottom.

"The beach is a terrific place for kite flying, of course, because there's no danger of getting tangled in kite-eating trees or television antennas or dangerous power lines," she explained. "However, people often use the more artistic kites for decoration rather than flying. Tell me if I'm pressing too hard or doing anything wrong."

"You're not doing a single thing wrong."

She was working on his neck now, doing magical things to the tense cords that often knotted at the back of his head. Her fingertips moved into his hair, gently rotating the scalp. Luke had had a few professional massages by the masseur at his health club in Boston, and he knew that, technically, Cindy probably wasn't as good. Ah, but there was more than raw technique to a successful back rub, and no professional massage had ever made him feel as great. "I haven't flown a kite in years," he murmured.

"That's because you're a workaholic," she chided gently. She touched his ears with feathery strokes, and he swallowed and felt a little light-headed. "Don't you know you're supposed to take time to smell the roses...and fly the kites?"

"And while your back is turned, someone sticks a knife in it," he muttered. And yet his back hadn't been turned. No one had worked longer and harder hours at Marianna Mutual Funds than he had. In fact, those hours alone at the office had been one of the incriminating arguments used against him.

He felt Cindy's hands pause momentarily. Hastily, before she could ask questions, he added, "There's a place under my right shoulder blade that's really sore."

She moved to the spot he indicated, and he closed his eyes. At the moment the bitter, angry thoughts that had obsessed him for months no longer seemed so important. What was important was what the woman straddling his back was doing to him. If she was a woman, he thought dreamily. Maybe she was really an angel, because surely no one but an angel could work such magic. The relaxation was penetrating even deeper now, beyond muscles and nerves and bones, infiltrating the tension that went to his very soul. Her fingers nibbled along the sides of his neck, glided up to his temples and then moved down his back in a series of light, chopping motions.

When she reached his belt line, she took a moment to relax, more of her weight settling on his buttocks, and the impression of ethereal angel vanished. She was woman. All woman. Warm and solid and desirable. It took all of Luke's willpower not to turn over and hold her hard against him. He squeezed his eyes shut and tried to think of something casual and inconsequential to say, something that would take his mind off the muscles that definitely were not relaxing.

"You'll have to unfasten your pants."

For a moment Luke thought he hadn't heard right, that some male fantasy had come true before he'd even put it into clear thought. Then he realized what she meant, of course, but he couldn't resist saying teasingly, "I thought you'd never ask."

"You said your lower back bothered you, and I need to be able to reach the muscles farther down." Her tone was prim and a little reproving.

"Reach anywhere you like." He raised himself to unfasten the button on his pants, feeling her legs tighten as his body moved beneath her. He unfastened the zipper about halfway. She moved to his right side, and he felt her rather gingerly lower the pants a few inches on his hips.

"Do you know you have a small bruise here?" she asked.

"I backed into a stack of lumber at the mill a couple nights ago."

She gave the muscles below his belt line a rather hurried massage and then told him he could refasten his pants.

"Do your legs bother you?" she asked.

"Every muscle I have bothers me." He prudently didn't elaborate on the one that was bothering him most at the moment, but he knew he'd better not turn over, or it would be all too obvious.

She massaged the backs of his legs, using a stronger grip to reach through the heavy, corded fabric. The touch through the fabric was perhaps less effective as a healing massage, but it had no less effect on Luke's senses. *Me and my dumb promises,* he groaned inwardly. Yet he knew he wouldn't be there right now if he hadn't made those assurances, and he wouldn't betray her trust.

But he damn sure hadn't made any promises about future nights. . . .

Cindy squatted back on her heels, hands clasped loosely in front of her. "I guess that's about all I can do for you. Sometimes a foot massage helps distant muscles."

"We'll save that for another time. Just let me lie here and relax for a few minutes, okay?"

"Would you like some coffee?"

"No, I don't think I'll have time. Thanks, anyway."

Cindy hadn't made up the new bed yet, but she didn't want to go into the bedroom and have him think she was broadcasting provocative hints. Except for those one or two suggestive statements—and she'd practically invited those, she had to admit—he hadn't said or done anything out of line. Apparently he'd taken the massage at face value, as exactly what it was supposed to be, exactly what he'd asked for: a back rub to soothe sore muscles. He'd felt no male/female undercurrents, experienced no sly dartings of physical arousal.

Which was great, of course.

Too bad it hadn't left *her* as unaffected, Cindy thought ruefully.

She felt stirred up inside, exhilarated and excited and nervous all at the same time. . .the way a kite looked when a gust of wind took it on a wild swoop and climb. She made a pretense of straightening things in the room around him, all the time surreptitiously keeping one eye on the motionless form on the floor.

He was still on his stomach, legs spread, toes turned outward. He should have looked vulnerable lying there with his eyes closed. But he didn't. He looked dangerous. Not dangerous in the sense that she physically feared for her safety with him. No. Dangerous in the sense of an attractive package whose contents were unknown. Dangerous because, seeing him lying there, all solid, muscular male, made her think wild thoughts. What would happen if she went over and lay down beside him . . . or kissed the nape of his neck . . . and he turned over and took her in his arms . . .

"You haven't fallen asleep, have you?" she asked almost sharply, dismayed by the turn of her thoughts.

"Do I get to stay the night if I have?" he murmured from within the pillow of his arms.

"You have to go to work."

He sat up, long legs crossing Indian fashion. "Yeah. The siren call of the lumber mill." The words came out on a wry sigh. He reached for his shirt and slipped it around his shoulders.

His pants were still unbuttoned, and she averted her eyes from the flash of white shorts. "Maybe, once you get a little seniority, you can transfer to day shift."

He shrugged as if he didn't really care one way or the other. "It's just a job. It doesn't much matter when I do it."

He buttoned the shirt, then stood up and turned away from her to tuck the shirttails into his pants. He grabbed his jacket from where he'd tossed it on a chair.

"Sounds as if it's raining now," he said.

"Rain is lousy for the kite business. Think *wind*."

"I'll do that."

"And I hope...I mean, you really are welcome to come into the kite shop anytime. You might find it interesting."

She followed him to the door, not quite certain what came next. How did one end a dinner-cum-massage date?

"Thanks for dinner and helping put my new bed together and everything," she offered on a tentative note.

"Thank you . . . for everything." He rotated his shoulders tentatively. His hair had grown tousled while he was lying down, taking a year or two off his almost intimidatingly handsome face. "I feel much better. Perhaps you should add a back rub sideline to your kite business."

Not if all her "clients" made her feel the way Luke had tonight, Cindy thought silently.

She thought he was going to walk out without touching her, and she was balancing relief with disappointment, when he reached out and ran his hand beneath her hair, lifting the pale blond strands from the nape of her neck.

"Do you ever wear your hair up like this?"

Cindy hesitated. "I suppose I have. Why?"

"No reason. It's very lovely hair, up or down." He rested his forearms on her shoulders and kissed her on the nose. "Is cinnamon addictive?" he asked.

"I don't know."

"I think it . . . or she . . . could be." He combed his fingers through her hair, pulling her head back a little as he did so, until her mouth was poised for his kiss. "I think a man could become so addicted to the taste of Cinnamon that he'd never want to leave."

Cindy swallowed. Her mind seemed to be doing peculiar loops and spins. "You . . . you have to get to work."

"I know." He dipped his head but, instead of kissing her full on the lips, merely brushed the corner of her mouth. "Good night, sweet bed partner. I'll be thinking of you."

Then he was gone, and Cindy was standing there with wind and rain in her face, foolishly holding the door open. She managed a wave at the retreating headlights and then closed the door.

It was several minutes before she realized that, in spite of his sweet talk about addiction to cinnamon, he hadn't said a word about seeing her again.

3

HE HADN'T, Cindy reflected, even mouthed that notorious goodbye line, "I'll call you."

She juggled relief and disappointment. She was attracted to him, no doubt about that. She yearned to make him laugh, to erase the somber wariness reflected in his dark eyes, to caress his angular cheeks. She was aware of explicitly centered yearnings of a far more physical nature. She could still taste the delicious expectation of the kiss she hadn't received.

She picked up the blanket he'd been lying on, absent-mindedly cuddling its fuzzy softness to her cheek to catch any lingering warmth from his body. But there was no warmth, just a faint scent of minty lotion. Then, realizing what she was doing, she briskly folded the blanket and returned it and the foam rubber mat to the closet.

She made up the new bed, showered and crawled between the fresh sheets. The new mattress felt good, not too hard, not too soft. No lumps and bumps, no downhill sag. She closed her eyes. Yet she lay there, her mind churning restlessly, wondering about Luke.

His nondescript apartment and classy little car clashed, like sneakers with a European-tailored suit. And the closetful of expensive suits clashed with the millworker's job. She didn't think he'd told her any outright lies, but he was so close-mouthed that he hadn't actually told her much of anything. She had the definite feeling that Luke Townsend wasn't exactly what he appeared to be, that he was concealing more than he revealed.

Yet even that uneasy suspicion couldn't erase the seductive memory of his warm, lean body clamped between her thighs, or dim her remembrance of the intriguing line of demarcation between his lightly tanned back and the pristine white skin below. The small rumbles of pleasure he made as her hands massaged his back...and the odd little shiver when she touched his ears.

She wondered why she'd done that. That feathery touch was no standard accompaniment to a back rub. She had deliberately, if at that moment subconsciously, tried to arouse some other reaction from him.

IN THE MORNING, dressed in bikini panties and bra, she went through her standard set of conditioning and flexibility exercises. Side and forward stretches, touching head beyond knees, push-ups and sit-ups, stretches in the split position. She occasionally regretted that she didn't have a barre, the rail at which all ballerinas worked out, but she could still do the five basic positions of the feet, pliés and a few arabesques and pirouettes her mother had taught her, if she was careful not to clunk into furniture. Gymnastics and ballet were more closely related than many people realized, although nowadays she did the exercises merely to keep fit, not as a preliminary to the gymnastics that had once followed. She felt no twinges in her knee, which pleased her. Sometimes she paid in pain for those urges that took her to the deserted beach for a rendezvous with her past, but there had been no bad aftereffects from the vigorous exercise of a few nights before.

Cindy half expected Luke to wander into the kite store that morning before he went home to sleep. When he didn't, she hoped he might come in later in the day, after he woke up. He didn't show up then, either. Nor did he appear the following day.

Cindy thought she was being discreet watching for him, but apparently she wasn't, because Joanna Stark, one of her salesclerks, finally said curiously the following morning, "Who in the world are you watching for? Every time the door opens you get a starry-eyed, expectant expression, and then some innocent customer walks in, and your face drops as if he were here to repossess your pickup."

"I . . . met someone. I thought he might drop by."

"Ah, a man." Joanna nodded knowingly. "I see. Want to tell Mama all about it?"

Joanna was two years younger than Cindy's twenty-six, but she was newly married and even more newly pregnant, playing and enjoying her pending mother role to the hilt.

Cindy had been absentmindedly folding an advertisement into a paper airplane, and she tartly aimed and tossed it in the direction of Joanna's slim midsection. "Mama, indeed," she scoffed. "How many hours pregnant are you now?"

Joanna ignored the question. "If you'll describe this man to me, I'll watch for him, too, and then you won't have to risk breaking your neck rushing to see who's at the door every time it opens."

Cindy sputtered indignantly. "I don't—" But then she remembered that a few minutes earlier she *had* nearly entangled herself in the carousel display of colorful wind socks. "Just look for the most handsome man you've ever seen," she advised flippantly. "One who makes you feel as if electric fingers walk up and down your spine when he looks at you."

"But I'm married to *him*," Joanna pointed out serenely.

Cindy avoided watching the door after that. Luke had given her no reason to believe he would see her again; he had, in fact, made a point of saying he didn't want to be involved with people, and that probably included her. Yet in spite of that dismal thought, both curiosity and concern about him niggled at the back of her mind. He could be sick . . . injured at work . . . maybe he'd even picked up and left town already. He hadn't sounded anchored here, or anywhere.

On impulse, she decided to lunch at the Chowder House. She assured herself that she wasn't deliberately planning to corner Jake Bennett and ply him with questions, but she might just casually inquire about Luke.

After dawdling over a bowl of chowder, adding a piece of blackberry pie, calling Joanna to say she'd be late and drinking innumerable cups of coffee, Cindy finally managed to "run into" Jake Bennett when he came to eat a meal with Cece. Cindy was gradually working around to the subject of Luke when Cece, bless her, saved her the trouble.

"Oh, I meant to ask Jake if he knew that guy you were in here with the other night. The big, good-looking one. You said he worked night shift at the mill. What was his name? Luke something."

"Townsend," Cindy filled in. She looked at Jake cautiously, not wanting to appear overeager for information.

"Luke? Oh, yeah. The new guy on the green chain. Hell of a hard worker. The first night just about did him in, and I didn't figure he'd last the week, but he toughened up fast. I don't think I'd want to be in a brawl with him. Not unless he was on my side."

"He's still working at the mill, then?" Cindy asked.

Jake drained his coffee cup and held it out to his wife for a refill. "Well, we got this flu going around—"

"He's sick?" Alarm surged through Cindy, surprising her with its intensity.

"Nah. But a lot of our men have been off work. We thought we might have to shut down, but enough volunteered for double or alternate shifts to keep us going. I think Luke has been working eight hours on, eight off, then another eight on."

Cindy stopped squeezing her coffee cup as if she were trying to mold it into a different shape. "Do you know him very well?" she asked, taking pride in her oh-so-casual tone of voice.

"Not really. He's pretty much of a loner. Doesn't have much to say. Not the kind of guy to stand around and shoot the bull at break time."

"He's unfriendly?"

"Well, no, I wouldn't say that exactly. He just kind of keeps to himself. But then men don't band together to do everything from shopping to going to the john the way you women do."

Cece punched him in the shoulder. "Male chauvinist."

Jake grinned. "And proud of it."

Cindy stopped herself from thanking Jake for the information about Luke, but she suspected she hadn't been fooling anyone when Cece called after her, "Don't worry, hon, Luke hasn't been in here with anyone else."

On the drive back to the shop, she had to laugh at herself. Here she'd been imagining deep, mysterious secrets about Luke, and all the time he was merely doing what workaholics usually did: working. Mill work wasn't something he could take home with him, so he'd simply volunteered to stay longer at the mill when the opportunity arose.

Of course, the fact that he apparently preferred working to pursuing a relationship with her wasn't exactly flattering or encouraging. She sighed ruefully. Still, she was relieved, and devoting oneself single-mindedly to some endeavor was something Cindy knew all about. She was as familiar with putting in long, dedicated hours, shutting out the rest of the world, as she was with sore muscles.

Did she want to become involved with a man like that? Not really. But people could change. She had. She'd once been so dedicated to a goal that she'd had no time for anything else.

She also knew you couldn't just grab someone like that and shove fun and relaxation down his throat.

Still, where a man couldn't be forced, perhaps he could be lured....

LUKE SLOGGED THROUGH THE SHIFT. He was beginning to lose track of how many eight hours on, eight hours off periods he'd worked. It was all beginning to get a little blurry.

Surprisingly, except for a blister he'd developed on his hand despite the protection of a leather glove, he didn't feel too bad physically. The body that he'd wanted to disown for the first few nights on the job had stopped cramping and complaining. Or maybe it was Cindy's rubdown that had really worked the magic. The memory of her touch and smile hit a soft place inside him that he'd thought long shriveled and dead.

He'd thought about her a lot these past few days. Not many women he knew could still blush peachy pink over something like his mild "bed partner" teasing. She was fun to be with, fun to tease, although her powers of observation were perhaps a little too keen for comfort.

His thoughts kept going back to that moment at her door, when he knew she'd expected him to kiss her. Lord knows he'd wanted to, but he hadn't dared. Not the way he'd already been feeling, vulnerable, with an ache that was part wanting to make love to her and part just wanting to hold her all night long. She was sweet and warm and infinitely desirable, a woman who stirred both his physical desire and a long-abandoned yearning for both love and companionship.

Yet what the hell would he do if he actually fell in love with her? Him with his tangled past and uncertain future, his rage and resentment and bitterness. No, love was an entanglement he didn't need. And commitment took more trust than he figured he'd ever be able to accumulate again.

Better just not to see her again.

When the shift was over, Luke sat in his car for a few minutes, head thrown back against the seat, before he could summon the energy to drive home. Once there, he fell into bed without bothering to fix anything to eat. All he could think of was that the flu epidemic was winding down and he didn't have to work that night. He had two—*two*—glorious nights off!

HE AWOKE ABOUT FOUR-THIRTY that afternoon. Nothing specific had wakened him, but he was aware of some small sound, an irregular whisper or rustle. Late-afternoon sunshine spilled through a crack in the draperies and threw a bright line across his navy-blue bedspread, while dust motes danced gently in the quiet air. He tried lazily to identify the sound but couldn't, although it did seem to be coming from the direction of the front door.

Finally he got up, threw on a robe and padded barefoot across the small living room. Something flopped into the room when he opened the door. A kite. An electric-yellow kite with a rainbow arched across it. It had been tied to the doorknob, and there was a note attached.

"You're working much too hard," the note read. "Have some fun! Go fly a kite and look for the rainbow."

There was no name, but Luke knew who had brought the kite, of course. "Look for the rainbow," he echoed wryly. That was like her, definitely a rainbow with every raindrop kind of woman. Sweet and lovely, with a naively optimistic outlook on life. She'd obviously never had her world jerked out from under her the way he had.

And suddenly he couldn't wait to see her again.

"THIS PLACE IS DEAD." Joanna stifled a yawn with one hand while she halfheartedly straightened a drooping serpent kite. "Mind if I leave a little early?"

Cindy looked at her watch and then the deserted street outside. Sunday afternoon business had been brisk earlier, but now the only movement out there was the flapping of the fifteen-foot green wind sock with the store's name on it and the whirling of the multicolored spinner-type wind socks beneath. "Go ahead. See you Tuesday?"

Challenge the Wind was open every day during the busy summer months but closed on Mondays at this time of year. Cindy usually also took one other day off during the week, leaving Joanna in charge. Now, after Joanna left, Cindy went back to the office to work on some charge card forms. The bell on the door jangled a few minutes later, just before closing time.

"Hi. Can I help— Luke!" Cindy hadn't planned to greet Luke quite so enthusiastically if he ever showed up at the kite shop, but it was too late now. That happy calling of his name was about as subtle as pouncing on him with a hug and kiss. She tried to salvage what she could with a guarded, "It's, uh, nice to see you again."

She threaded her fingers together, conscious of an inappropriate desire to reach out and stroke his freshly shaven cheek. He had a clean, slightly soapy fragrance, but her first thought was that he was far too good-looking and attractive to be as innocent as that scent implied.

"Nice to see you, too. I haven't had much free time. I've been putting in overtime at the mill. Thanks for the kite."

"You're welcome."

She tried not to be affected by the sight of him simply standing there with one hand casually braced on the counter. Men stood there all the time while they bought a kite or made conversation. Interesting men. Attractive men.

And not one of them had ever made her feel the way Luke Townsend did right now, this peculiar combination of adolescently shy and femininely restless. He was casually dressed in jeans and sweater, but the pale coral pullover looked like cashmere. With it, his dark hair and eyes...and warm smile...had the impact of an explosion waiting to happen. Maybe in her heart.

He glanced upward, toward the walls and high ceiling covered with a jumbled array of colorful kites. Others swung from carousel displays or hung suspended in midair in friendly clutters. "Interesting place. Is that invitation to look around still open?"

"Oh, of course!" Her answer was eager, but then she had the awkward feeling that perhaps he'd come because he felt obligated to do so, because of the kite at his door, not because he'd really wanted to see her again. She started showing him around, however, and within moments her enthusiasm for her work erased the uneasiness.

"These big triangular ones are called delta kites, the name actually coming from the Greek letter of the same name, of course. Deltas and the diamond shapes are our most popular kites, although, as you can see, kites come in practically every shape imaginable." She waved toward a rather evil-looking, black, bat-shaped kite with ruby-colored eyes.

Luke reached out and rubbed the bat's fabric between his fingers. "What are they made of?"

"Usually parachute nylon, although a few are ripstop nylon. The material has a grid pattern that won't tear if it's punctured. Parachute nylon does tend to fray, but I like it better because it looks so delicate and yet it's very strong. We also have some kites, particularly the large serpent and dragon styles, that are made of a plastic film."

"They're all gorgeous. Where do they come from?"

"Most of the inexpensive ones come from a wholesale import company. The others are designed and manufactured at the main Challenge the Wind store up in Astoria. This is actually a branch store." A little shyly she added, "I've designed a few of the kites myself."

"The ballerina kite on the wall at your cottage?"

Cindy nodded. She led him to another room off to the side, where the box kites were displayed by themselves because they took up so much space. Box kites were made of numerous smaller pieces of nylon fabric made into complicated, three-dimensional shapes, bulky but light and graceful. "That one is my favorite," she said, pointing to a star formed of red and pink triangles intricately fitted together around a fiberglass framework.

"I suppose kids are your biggest customers?" Luke asked.

"Oh, no. We get all ages. In fact, the stunt models and these larger box kites take a lot of strength and skill to fly, and some definitely aren't recommended for children. One like that—" Cindy pointed to an airy, colorful box kite taller than she was "—dragged me all over the beach the last time I took it out. I often take kites down to the beach for flying demonstrations. It's good for business." She smiled. "And lots of fun for me."

She finished by showing him the stunt and fighter kites. "The line on a fighter kite may be coated with abrasive material for about thirty feet back from the kite itself. The object of a contest with these is to cut your opponent's line and set his kite adrift."

Luke smiled, but his tone was a bit wry when he said, "Even the carefree world of kite flying is not all sweetness and light, I see. How did you ever get into this business?"

"I don't type. Computers confuse me. I make terrible tacos. I never learned brain surgery." Cindy smiled again. "What else could I do but go fly a kite?"

They were back at the cluttered counter near the main entrance by then. Luke laughed, a nice, friendly chuckle that did unlikely things to the pit of her stomach. Yet she had the feeling that he thought all this was a little frivolous, that her kites were lovely toys for people who had time for whimsical, time-wasting activities. Not for him.

"You didn't go fly the kite I left for you, did you?" Cindy asked.

"I really haven't had time. I just woke up an hour or so ago."

"But you don't intend to fly it, do you?"

"I thought I'd hang it on the wall, the way you have those at your cottage," Luke admitted. He leaned back against the counter, long legs crossed at the ankles. The delicate coral color of the sweater contrasted with the powerful span of his shoulders. He no longer moved as if he was stiff and sore. "It's very pretty. Delicate looking, but strong. Like you."

"It's made to fly. You can fly it and still hang it on the wall."

"Maybe I'll get around to flying it sometime."

"No, I don't think you will." Cindy folded her arms. In spite of her earlier eagerness to see him, in spite of feeling foolishly feminine in response to his aura of virility, she was oddly annoyed with him now. "Workaholics don't have time for just having fun. Flying a kite isn't making money or getting ahead in the world or improving yourself or making progress toward some big goal. It's just having fun. So you won't have time for it."

His gaze narrowed, as if he intended to strike back at her, but instead he said mildly, "You've pigeonholed my character and decided all this about me just because I put in a few hours' overtime at the mill?"

Cindy hesitated. Maybe she was unfairly jumping to conclusions. But she didn't think so. Perhaps she recognized a certain intensity or tension in him because she had once had it herself, a dedication to work so fierce that everything outside achieving a particular goal was scorned as a waste of time. "Okay, what do you do that's just for fun?" she challenged.

He looked as if he might tell her it was none of her business, but then said, "Well, I like to walk on the beach."

She recognized that it had taken him a moment to come up with an answer. "For the fun of it, or because you figure the exercise is good for you?"

He ignored the barb. "I like going out to dinner at a good restaurant. Seeing an occasional play or movie. Reading a good book. I watch television occasionally, especially football. I like to dance. I thought I might try windsurfing sometime." He hesitated, eyes glinting dangerously, and for a moment she thought he might arrogantly add sex to his list of fun pastimes. If so, he changed his mind, because he shrugged and said, "I guess that's it, unless you want to add jogging and racquetball. I used to enjoy them, even though I did them for the exercise. At the moment I get more than enough exercise on the job."

"And mostly you work. Right? I'll bet, before you were a mill worker, you were involved in something where you took piles of work home every night."

"What is this? You have something against hard work?" Luke's tone was still pleasant, but a note of hostility lurked beneath the mildness. His lean figure straightened, as if it wouldn't take much to make him stalk out.

Cindy frowned lightly. Attacking hard work was a little like criticizing mom and apple pie, and it wasn't really what she meant to do. "No, of course not. I work hard, too. I'm not advocating a life of laziness. I'm just for keeping work in a proper perspective. What did you do before you came to Steller Beach?"

The abrupt question took him by surprise. Then he startled her by answering rather than evading the question, although she was aware of a moment of tension before he decided to do so.

"I was connected with a mutual-funds group back East, the Marianna Mutual Funds. My fund specialized in energy-related stocks, and my particular area of expertise was with companies involved in solar and other alternative energy systems. I was assistant manager, and there were always financial reports and balance sheets to take home to study, when I didn't stay late at the office instead."

"Shifting from mutual funds to mill work seems a rather large jump. Why did you decide to change?"

He moved a shoulder in a casual, dismissive gesture. "Circumstances change. Actually, I came out here thinking I'd go to work on a fishing boat. When I was a kid my family came to the Oregon coast on a vacation one year. My dad and I went out on a charter boat, and I caught a big salmon. It was a real thrill. When I decided to . . . change careers, I thought I'd like to work on a fishing boat for a living. But when I got to the Oregon coast I discovered the fishing business was in a slump. There weren't any jobs even for experienced men, let alone for someone like me." He laughed ruefully. "So much for basing a career change on the memory of a twelve-year-old who once caught a fish. So now I pull green chain in a lumber mill."

"Is it just a temporary change? You still read *The Wall Street Journal* to keep up on what's going on in the world of stocks and bonds."

"How did you know that?"

"There was a copy of it on your coffee table."

"You're very observant." He didn't sound as if he particularly appreciated that trait and abruptly changed the subject, ending the brief flow of information about himself. "How do you like your new bed by now?"

"It's quite comfortable." She felt rather *un*comfortable discussing that subject with him, however. She'd had a shockingly intimate dream in that bed one night, a dream in which Luke had played a starring role. It was not one of those forgotten-on-awakening dreams, and she hoped he was no mind reader. "How about yours?"

"Just fine. Makes me think of you every time I crawl into it."

Cindy tried to keep the color from flowing into her face, but from his lazy smile she knew she hadn't been successful.

"You have a lovely blush. Makes you look about sixteen."

She also wasn't successful in warding off a vivid mental image of Luke slipping into his own bed. He was not, she suspected, a pajama man. At least not in her image. She was the one to abruptly change the subject this time. "How's your back?"

"Much better, thank you. No more muscle cramps in the chest, either. If you'll have dinner with me, you won't have to pay for it with a back rub this time."

Cindy's earlier feeling of awkwardness returned. "I didn't give you the kite with the idea of making you feel obliged to . . . to reciprocate in some way." She hoped she was telling the truth. "I just thought it would be nice if you did something relaxing and enjoyable, something fun. You do seem . . . tense." She said the last word rather lamely, because it didn't express all that she sensed about him. There was a smolder of something she couldn't quite define, a hint of volatile explosiveness. A ready alertness, as if he didn't intend to be caught with defenses down. He hadn't, she realized, actually explained why he'd decided to make such an abrupt career change, except for that enigmatic comment, "Circumstances change."

"I started out without too many advantages in life," was his response to her expression of concern. "I wanted to get ahead, and I was willing to work to do it. I don't suppose fun has had a very high priority in my life." He smiled lightly at the admission, but didn't sound as if he intended to change his ways.

"Maybe you ought to kind of ease into fun then." Cindy's blue eyes sparkled; ideas were beginning to form. "Sneak up on it."

He folded his arms across his chest. "And how does one ease into having fun?" he inquired. "Set aside five minutes a day the first week, work up to ten minutes—"

"No, no." Cindy impatiently rejected his facetious suggestion. "You do something that on the surface looks like work but is really fun. You said you believed in self-sufficiency, didn't you?"

"What do you know about self-sufficiency?" Luke scoffed. He sounded tolerantly amused when he added, "I'll bet the biggest problem you've ever had in your life is feeling guilty about all the hearts you've broken. How many guys did you have to turn down for your senior prom?" He reached out and stroked her jaw with fingertips roughened by hard work.

Cindy gave him an odd glance that suddenly made her look older than her years, and the vivacious sparkle in her eyes turned brittle as she stepped away from the touch of his hand. "Actually, I never went to a senior prom." Nor had she participated in many of the other carefree activities most girls enjoyed in their teen years.

She had also never had time for broken hearts. Her relationship with Jeff had dragged out so long and so loosely that it had ended with sighs of resignation more than tears. "I wasn't talking about emotional self-sufficiency," she said.

"What, then?"

"When I first came here to the coast I also encountered some difficulties making a living. So I learned a few points about *real* self-sufficiency. Living off the land, or sea, in this case."

"Really?" Luke looked surprised. His gaze ran over her again, an inspection that probed beneath the honey-tan skin and willowy curves.

Cindy fumbled through the clutter on the counter and finally came up with the sheet she was looking for. She ran her finger down the list of dates and times. "Mmm, I thought so. There's a minus tide tomorrow morning—oh, but it's too early! You'll be at work."

"I have two nights off." Tilting his head, he added, "And if I'm so devoted to work and such a confirmed workaholic, how come I'm so happy about that?"

"Maybe you're making progress already." She went back to the fine print schedule of high and low tide times. "Let's see, low tide is seven forty-three, and we ought to be there an hour before that—"

"What are you mumbling about?"

He stepped around behind her so he could look at the schedule. He clasped her shoulders lightly, and his jaw brushed her hair. The touch was distracting, and she was glad she had already located the necessary tide figure, because now the numbers all seemed to run together.

"I was figuring what time we should be down at the beach in the morning."

"To do what?"

"To go clamming. A minus tide means an exceptionally low tide with more beach exposed, so it's a good time for digging clams. And clamming is an activity that ought to suit you just fine. It's free food, and it's hard work. That and getting up at five-thirty in the morning should be enough to convince the workaholic part of you that what we're doing isn't really for fun."

"Are we doing it for fun?" he asked doubtfully.

"Wait and see," she suggested. "You'll need old clothes, something you don't mind getting sandy and wet. We'll go in my pickup so you won't get your car dirty. Let's see, I'll have to locate my clamming shovels and a couple of burlap bags—" Suddenly Cindy realized she was pushing this rather brashly, and she immediately backed off. "Of course, if you'd rather not . . ."

He turned her to face him. "I'm going to get up at some ungodly hour of the morning, rush out to get cold, dirty and wet, after which, if we're successful, I suspect there will be some messy, clam-cleaning chores. How could I possibly turn down an invitation to participate in such irresistible activities?"

"You're sneaking up on fun. It's kind of . . . fun in disguise."

He laughed. "Well disguised, I'd say."

"If you really don't want to—"

"I wouldn't miss it for the world. Especially when I'm going to have such a lovely teacher." His grip tightened on her arms. His smile reached his eyes, warming the brown with amber lights.

"Very well, then, we should meet at—"

"First I want to give you a little present I brought you. It's out in the car. Isn't it about time for you to close up here?"

It was well past regular closing time by then. "Why—why would you bring me a present?"

"Why not?" he countered.

"Couldn't you bring the present in here?"

"It's a bit . . . mmm . . . personal. Might cause speculation if a customer wandered in." He smiled at her look of curiosity mixed with uneasiness. "C'mon, I'll help you close up. What do you have to do?"

She directed him to check a side door and turn off some lights while she took care of the cash register. She secured the main door, and he touched her elbow lightly to guide her to his car as they stepped onto the sidewalk.

She stopped short, turning so that her hand caught his arm. "Luke, I really wish you hadn't done this. Just because I gave you the kite doesn't mean—"

"I know. But anyone can give anyone a kite." He smiled, and the teasing grin and the ruffling of the wind in his hair gave him a look that was both enchantingly wicked and carelessly innocent. "But what I have for you is a present I'd share only with a bed partner."

4

CINDY PEERED into the bulky sack on the seat of the Alfa Romeo. "A pillow!"

"The one that came with my apartment was all flat and hard, and I noticed yours wasn't much better. So I stopped downtown and bought a matching pair... to go with our matching beds."

The gift was a shade intimate, considering their short acquaintance, but Cindy was so relieved that it wasn't something even more intimate, perhaps a scrap of lacy bedtime lingerie, that she didn't protest.

"Of course it comes with one, mmm, qualification," Luke warned.

Cindy had been squeezing the pillow, approving its springy feel. She jerked back her hand as if she'd just discovered hot rocks in the cloud-soft filling. She was standing within the angle formed by the open car door, while Luke held the door open against the whip of the wind. His body and spread arms also effectively blocked her retreat.

"Qualification?"

"It's been programmed to encourage sweet dreams about the giver."

Again Cindy had been expecting something more suggestive, and her laugh held a ripple of relief. "I very seldom dream," she said quickly. "But it's a useful and very lovely gift. Thank you."

"Do you want to take it with you now, or should I bring it over later when I pick you up for dinner? Or would you like to go to dinner right now?"

He had obviously assumed she would have dinner with him, but if he was surprised when Cindy said she already had plans for the evening, he was too controlled to show more than a tightening of the fine lines around his mouth.

"Then I'll see you in the morning. What time?"

"Be at my place about a quarter of six. I'll have breakfast ready. The best clamming beach is about a half hour's drive, so we can be there by quarter of seven. The tide will still be going out."

"My early arrival won't . . . interrupt anything?"

Cindy picked up her new pillow and said airily, "Only my sweet dreams."

Yet as she sat in her own car and watched Luke drive away, she halfway wished she'd been more forthright. Of course she did date occasionally, but that evening's plans were merely a promise to baby-sit her landlady's children. Luke's assumption that she was seeing another man hadn't made him back off, but she'd sensed a certain strengthening of that familiar barrier of reserve, and regretted that her actions had caused it.

She located the tools they'd need for the following morning and stashed them in the pickup before going to Denise Barberry's home. She was back and in bed by ten o'clock, head nestled into the soft comfort of her new pillow as she wondered what Luke was doing at that hour. If he'd wanted feminine companionship for the evening, he probably hadn't had any difficulty finding it.

LUKE'S COMPANION AT THAT MOMENT was indeed a ravishing, bikini-clad redhead—but she was speaking to him from the television screen about the marvelous qualities of a soft drink, and he was paying no attention either to her words or her lithe body. He was studying the stock market section of a Portland newspaper, noting that prices on several stocks he'd chosen for the Marianna Energy Fund were up considerably. The knowledge gave him mixed feelings: satisfaction that his judgment had proved correct but anger and resentment that the mutual fund responsible for his bitterness was the beneficiary.

He started to crumple the page, then smoothed it and studied the columns again. He knew exactly how he'd invest a fund's money right then if he were in command, noting from long experience where ripe opportunities lay in several stocks that were strong yet currently underpriced. Maybe he shouldn't have come out here and cut himself off from the exciting challenges of that world. Perhaps he should have tried to get a job with a different mutual fund, looked for a fresh opportunity....

No.

That part of his life was over and done with. There were no opportunities for him in that world. The injustice of it burned like acid in his mouth, and this time he did crumple the page and hurl it at the wastepaper basket, angry with himself for even looking at it.

He showered and slid into bed, not sleepy but aware that five-thirty would come quickly. The new pillow felt good, soft but springy. He folded his arms behind his head and thought about Cindy, wondering if she was with some other man. Even though he found the thought vaguely disturbing, he reminded himself that her activities were none of his concern. He probably should have rejected outright this crazy idea of chasing after clams with her at the crack of dawn. He'd offered dinner, and she'd turned it down, and that fulfilled any obligation he might have in return for the gift of the kite.

Then he had to smile in the darkness at her idea of sneaking up on fun, as if it were some furry little creature you could throw a net over and capture. She was such a cheerful, lighthearted person, if perhaps a bit naive in her optimism. Except for those odd, fleeting moments when some bleak thought seemed to cross her mind....

Yet when the alarm went off at five-thirty, it was with a sense of anticipation more than obligation that he stumbled out of bed.

"HI! HOPE YOU LIKE pancakes and scrambled eggs."

"Coffee, woman. I need coffee." Luke exaggerated a bleary-eyed look and put out a hand as if feeling his way through the door. At this hour of the morning the scent of fresh coffee permeating the kitchen was more seductive than the most expensive perfume.

Cindy laughed and thrust a steaming cup into his hand. She was dressed in faded jeans and a gray sweatshirt that matched the color of the old warm-up outfit he wore under a heavy jacket. With no makeup and her hair tied back with a twist of pink yarn, she looked as innocent as a just wakened angel. But the kind of angel a man might like to take back to bed and snuggle up to . . .

She was all business, however, as she planted a man-size stack of pancakes and maple-flavored syrup in front of him. "We don't want to be late."

Privately Luke wasn't too sure about that, but over the quick meal he inquired if there was anything he should know about the sport of clamming. "Don't the clams object to this invasion of their early-morning privacy, perhaps mount a counterattack or something?" If he were a clam, he figured he could find a lot to object to.

Cindy laughed. "No, they don't attack. But they aren't called razor clams for nothing. The shells can be sharp, so be careful."

"And a minor cut—something that requires no more than a half dozen or so stitches—that's just part of the fun, right?" She made a face at him and started filling a stainless steel vacuum bottle with coffee.

They were on their way just a few minutes later, snug in the warm cab of the little pickup with early-morning fog thick around them. The dirt road turnoff to the beach some miles north of town wasn't marked, but Cindy apparently had no difficulty recognizing it.

"Hey, I thought we'd be here alone, but people are all over the place." Luke looked in surprise at the lineup of at least a dozen vehicles, with another car following them down the rough road. On the beach, ghostly shapes of people who had arrived earlier materialized here and there as the mist shifted in the erratic breeze.

"A minus tide brings lots of people out."

Luke followed Cindy to the rear of the pickup. She handed him a peculiar-looking shovel, long and narrow, and a burlap bag.

"We're each allowed twenty-four clams." She slipped a pair of knee-high rubber boots over her shoes and tucked her pant legs inside.

Luke eyed the surf-washed beach and felt the mist bead his skin with chill moisture. He thought with a certain longing of his comfortable new bed and pillow. "Wouldn't it be easier if I just took you out for a clam dinner tonight?" he asked plaintively.

Cindy ignored the suggestion. "If you don't want to get your shoes wet, you'd better leave them here."

"I'll just wear them, thank you. I imagine squishing around in wet shoes is part of the 'fun.'"

She started out at a brisk walk, heading toward the wide expanse of flat beach exposed by the retreating tide. Occasional higher waves still rolled over the sand, leaving a silvery film of water. People stood around, staring intently at the sand, until suddenly one would start digging frantically. It was all a mystery to Luke.

Cindy was watching the ground now, too. Suddenly she jammed her shovel in the sand, and he had to jump aside to avoid the flying debris as she dug. A moment later she was on her knees, reaching into the hole. Then Luke was astonished to see her flat on her stomach, squirming to reach deeper.

She bounced up, hand raised in triumph. "Clam!" she announced.

The clam was a brownish oval about five inches long, not particularly appetizing looking in its present condition.

"There! Start digging right there!" Cindy pointed to a slight indentation in the sand, and Luke obediently started digging. When he had a hole some two feet deep he reached down and felt around inside it.

"Nothing," he announced, privately not too surprised.

"You can't dig as if you're planting petunias and have all day." She sounded exasperated. "You have to dig *fast*."

"Why?"

"Because if you don't, the clam digs faster than you do and gets away."

Luke looked at the motionless lump in the burlap sack. "You're telling me that—that clam thing can dig faster than I can?" He felt almost insulted, as if his manhood had been belittled.

"A razor clam can dig down a foot or so per minute. If it's already fairly deep in the sand, you're not apt to catch up."

Up to this point, Luke hadn't felt there was any particular challenge involved in going after some inert shell buried in the sand beneath his feet, but suddenly he realized this was not necessarily so. Apparently he had just been outwitted.

He picked up the shovel with new determination. "How do I know where to dig?"

"You watch for a little indentation in the sand. If you don't see one, it sometimes helps to do this."

Cindy stomped the sand in an energetic little dance, hair flying, then peered at the sand around her. "Do you see anything? Pounding the sand makes a clam pull in its neck and creates a dimple in the sand."

But Luke was looking at Cindy, not the sand. She'd already lost the yarn in her hair, and the blond strands looked like tangled streaks of sunshine in the swirling mist. Her middle and bottom were sand covered, her legs shapeless in the oversize rubber boots, and she looked more like a disreputable tomboy than an innocent angel. No glamour, no sophistication, traits Luke had always thought he preferred in a woman. And yet at this moment he had the strangest desire to throw down his shovel, swing her up in his arms and kiss her.

Cindy glanced up at him, frowning at his lack of activity. "What are you looking at?"

"I guess I never saw anyone do a clam dance before."

"It's practically the favorite pastime here. There, right at your feet!" she cried, pointing to a nearly imperceptible pitting of the sand.

Luke dug, not expertly but fast, and when he reached into the hole he came up gleefully waving a sand-covered clam. "I got it!"

After that he still had some failures, empty holes that produced nothing more than a disappointing handful of wet sand, but usually he had a clam to add to the burlap bag. His arm was longer than Cindy's, so he didn't have to get down on his stomach the way she sometimes did, but by the time the tide turned he was as dirty and wet as she was. They hadn't gotten their limit, but the burlap bags were heavy when they carried them back to the pickup—and Luke's was heavier than Cindy's.

Luke poured coffee from the vacuum bottle she'd brought and curled his hands gratefully around the warmth of the cup. "Now what?"

"Now, as you suspected, there are cleaning chores." She smiled at his grimace.

"No," he said decisively. "Now we go home and shower and change clothes. First things first."

The morning fog had almost burned away by the time they got back to Cindy's cottage. Luke left a souvenir of damp sand on the seat and floorboards when he slid out of the pickup.

"Did you bring a change of clothes?" Cindy asked.

"No."

"Too bad. If you had, you could have showered and changed here." She smiled cheerfully as she dangled the lost opportunity like a prize just out of reach.

"Don't you have an old bathrobe or something I could wear until my clothes dried?"

"Nope."

"I'm not fussy. Old towel? Sheet?"

"Sorry. But if you want to bring your dirty clothes when you come back, we'll run them down to the Laundromat."

WHILE HE WAS GONE Cindy started the cleaning process by putting the clams in a tub of fresh water and adding a couple of tablespoons of cornmeal. She'd showered and changed into fresh jeans and shirt by the time he returned. They took their sandy, wet clothes to the Laundromat, then returned to the cottage to complete the cleaning. Cindy had intended to suggest that in the afternoon they fly Luke's new kite but perversely, the wind chose not to blow. Instead they spent a companionable afternoon strolling around the boat basin, watching a few scattered fishing boats come in, tossing the remnants of a sack of popcorn they'd bought to the squabbling gulls. Later they wandered up to the town's small park. Cindy sat in a swing, and Luke idly pushed her as they talked.

Cindy was pleased that Luke seemed so relaxed, more open and at ease with her than he'd been before. The swing reminded him of one he'd had when he was a boy, and he laughed as he reminisced about his boyhood ambition to make that swing go up, up and over the limb it was tied to.

"And here I thought you were probably a budding stockbroker by the age of ten, saving your pennies to invest in IBM," she teased.

"And how about you? What was your girlhood ambition?"

Cindy hesitated, caught in a momentary trap of guilt. She wanted Luke to be open and honest with her, to share a past that she sensed had been more than a little rocky, and yet she wasn't being totally open with him. She could tell him about the ambition that had engrossed her for years, the hard work and disappointments and heartaches and the final failure.... Yet who wanted to hear all that depressing stuff that no longer mattered?

Instead she chose to bring up a different, totally unrelated memory, deliberately choosing something she thought would make him smile. "When I was small I read a story about a little girl who had an invisible friend, and what I wanted most was to be that invisible friend. I thought of all the wonderful fun we could have, all the pranks I could pull if no one could see me. Once I sat in my closet for most of an afternoon trying to will myself into becoming invisible." She chuckled ruefully. "Of course now I suppose some child psychologist would read all sorts of ominous warnings into the wish of a little girl like that."

Luke held the swing to stop its motion, his lips close enough to tingle her ear as he murmured into it. "I'm glad you didn't succeed. It would be a shame if someone so lovely was invisible."

They went back to the cottage when it was time to prepare dinner. Cindy dipped the clams in her own special homemade batter, fried them to crispy, delicious tidbits and served them with a spicy sauce. Luke said he'd never tasted anything better and consumed enough to prove it.

Afterward, feeling well fed and languorous, they took a leisurely walk along a moonlit trail behind the cottage. A scent of wood smoke from a nearby fireplace lingered in the air, blending with other scents of pine and fir and damp earth. Hands joined, they walked in companionable silence to the end of the trail at a flat rock on a bluff that overlooked the ocean. A camp fire on the beach made a glowing pinpoint of light, insignificant beneath the glory of the moon.

Houses were nearby, but the barrier of trees and undergrowth of brambles and ferns gave the rock a peaceful seclusion. Luke sat with his elbows braced on his knees, one of her hands clasped between both of his. Night noises filtered out of the darkness, rustles and whispers and chirps, unidentifiable but not unfriendly.

"Bored?" Cindy asked finally when the silence stretched out.

He turned to look at her in the silvery light. "Why would you think that?"

"It's been a quiet day. Just you and me . . . walking and talking. Not what you're used to, I think."

"I didn't come out here to continue what I was accustomed to. I came to find something . . . different."

"What?"

"Maybe you."

"That sounds like a line, Luke Townsend. Don't give me phony singles bar lines." Her voice came out low and a little fierce, more emotional than she intended.

"I'm sorry if it sounded that way. That wasn't how I meant it."

The apology sounded sincere enough, but he was looking at her so intently that she stirred restlessly on the hard rock. "Why are you looking at me like that?"

As he had done once before, he scooped her hair away from her face and lifted it to the back of her head. He studied the result. "Sometimes you remind me of someone. Especially in the moonlight."

"Someone special?" she asked, uneasy at the thought.

"I don't know. I never met her."

"That's a strange thing to say. How could I remind you of her if you never met her?"

He rearranged the pale halo of hair, coiling it around one finger at the back of her head, so engrossed that he seemed not to hear her question. His hands were roughened by work, and the silky strands caught on the rough places. It was not an unpleasant feeling. It made her want to snuggle her cheek into that rough hand even as she wondered at the strangeness of his actions.

"Sometimes I think there's more to you than the carefree kite flyer you pretend to be," he mused with a little frown. He turned her face to study it in profile.

For a moment Cindy was tempted to explore that unexpected insight, but instead she tossed her head, sending the fragile coil he had created tumbling around her shoulders. "Of course I'm more than a kite flyer." She pretended a touch of indignation. "I'm also a clam digger, fairly good cook—"

"Terrific cook. But a second-rate clam digger," he proclaimed, smiling with teasing superiority. "I dug more of them than you did."

"Beginner's luck," she scoffed.

"We'll see. What other sneak-up-on-fun projects do you have in mind?"

"Did you really have fun today?" Cindy asked a little hesitantly.

"I really had fun today," he assured her.

"I have to work tomorrow—"

"Now who's the workaholic?" he challenged.

"But if there's a good wind I'm going to take one of the new stunt kites down to the beach after lunch and try it out."

"I'll be there."

"Bring your kite," she suggested.

"I'll think about it."

He was still looking at her, and finally she said, "I suppose we should be going." She started to stand up.

His hand clamped around her shoulder and held her down. "If you think you're going to lure me to a romantic spot like this and then rush me off without a kiss, think again."

She started to deny that she had "lured" him anywhere, but instead whispered more honestly, "I was beginning to think you hadn't noticed what a romantic spot it was."

Luke chuckled. He framed her face with his palms, tender in their touch. His gaze roamed her upturned, moonlit face, his own features in shadow. He touched the corners of her mouth with his thumbs, pulling her lips lightly against her teeth. Cindy held her breath, as if breathing might shatter the moment. Several times during the day she had thought he was going to kiss her and each time he hadn't, and she was half afraid he would change his mind again.

He didn't. His hands tightened around her face, then slid into her hair. She felt the gleam of moonlight against her closed eyelids, and then his shadow cut off the light. He made a husky sound when their lips met. He ran his tongue along the parted opening of her mouth, as if seeking the sweet cinnamon spice of her name.

Cindy returned the tentative exploration, and his arms went around her. He pulled her to her feet and arched her body against his own as the kiss deepened.

She didn't resist, and her body melted into the muscular lines of his. She was already hungry for his kiss, appetite heightened by the times she'd anticipated a kiss during the day and hadn't received it. But it had been worth waiting for....

His lips were soft but strong, tongue warm and exciting, tempting more than demanding.

She felt a pent-up hunger in him that went even deeper than her own, as if the kiss were releasing an urgency hitherto held on a leash. The probe of his tongue deepened, and the hunger went from controlled restraint to a blaze of desire. His lips left hers and moved to her closed eyelids, temples, cheeks. His hands slid beneath her jacket and blouse and found bare skin. His palms felt momentarily cold against her heated skin, but the small shiver that went through her was not one of objection to his touch. The night sounds faded away, and she was conscious only of a pounding in her ears that was more feeling than sound, as though the distant surf were surging through her.

His lips circled her mouth in a rain of small kisses, but when they moved to reclaim her mouth, she touched two fingers against them.

"Luke..." she whispered, softly, helplessly, wanting his kiss with her mouth, wanting more with her body, yet knowing in her mind that she wasn't yet ready for the point of no return that just one more kiss might lead to. She was that close to sinking to the ground, drawing him with her, making wild love beneath the drench of moonlight.

Her fingers trembled against his lips, then started to fall, but he caught and held them there. He kissed them tenderly.

"I know," he whispered.

No anger or insistence, no seductive persuasion—and that understanding "I know" was almost more difficult for Cindy to resist than some deliberately provocative overture would have been. Yet she was grateful that he didn't choose to test her resistance.

She took a shaky, steadying breath, then challenged him to a race down the trail. She grabbed a head start and, knowing each twist and turn, each branch and rock on the dark trail, won easily. He didn't kiss her again at the door, but just gave her an exaggerated little bow, acknowledging her victory. A moment later he was gone, red taillights that winked from the tree-lined driveway mocking her for the feeling of aloneness that swept over her in the darkness. Only a word or touch, and she knew she wouldn't have been alone. . . .

CINDY WAS ALREADY AT THE BEACH just below the town park when Luke arrived the following afternoon, and she'd already collected a small crowd of interested onlookers. Luke found a rock that offered a good vantage point.

The stunt kite was actually a series of colorful, ribbon-tailed kites held together with fine lines. He watched in admiration and not a little amazement as Cindy put the train of kites through its paces. She could make them climb and dive, loop in a series of a dozen dizzying spins, glide gracefully through one figure eight after another. The kites moved like a chorus line of precision dancers, gliding and dipping and whirling in unison, and the choreography all came from Cindy's expert hands. There was applause from the onlookers when she deliberately stalled the kite train and finally let it sink gracefully to the sand.

More important than the applause from a business point of view, Luke knew, were the admiring people who came forward to examine the kites, to ask where they could buy and learn to fly some like them. However, Luke admired Cindy for more than the way she'd made the kites dance with the wind. He liked the way she'd skillfully harnessed the wind's strength and power. *All this untamed energy going to waste,* he thought regretfully as the wind whipped his hair and pant legs and a stray paper plate scuttled by. When he'd been with Marianna Energy Fund, he'd dealt with the stock of a few companies that were making commercial use of wind power. And suddenly he had to laugh, because he knew his practical point of view about the wind would vex Cindy.

He wanted to wait until she was alone before approaching, and she was back at the pickup by the time the admiring onlookers finally dispersed. She was in pink shorts and short-cropped T-shirt, bare midriff and legs temptingly slim and lovely. He had to wonder if some of the men in the crowd hadn't been admiring something other than her kite flying.

"You're pretty darn good at that," he offered. "That really takes skill and experience."

She took instant notice that his hands were empty, of course, and ignored the compliments. "Where's your kite?"

"I guess I didn't bring it."

"Why not?" She answered the question for him. "Because you still think kite flying is kind of silly. Kid stuff. Undignified. A waste of time. Frivolous." She climbed into the back of the pickup with the train of colorful kites, careful not to tangle the lines. For the first time he noticed several fine whitish lines that looked like scars around one knee.

"You make a non-kite-flyer sound practically un-American."

She stopped what she was doing with the kites and looked at him. He thought she was going to make some angry retort, but instead, after a small narrowing of blue eyes, she unexpectedly laughed. "I keep forgetting what a novice you are at having fun, that we're still teaching you how to sneak up on it."

"I'm ready for another sneak attack whenever you are."

"We'll know we've succeeded when you're able to come down here and just fly your kite, unconcerned that you're not doing a thing but enjoying yourself. Do you think you'll ever reach that point?" she asked seriously.

Luke smiled. "Maybe." But privately he doubted it. Kite flying was not for him . . . but he wasn't so certain the same was true of this lovely kite flyer, who bumped his shoulder with a shapely curve of derriere as she climbed out of the back of the pickup.

THEY CARVED OUT TIME to be together, juggling the conflict of mismatched days off and different sleeping and working hours. They sneaked up on fun in strange and sometimes uncomfortable ways, always with some tangible result to show for their efforts so that, as Cindy said, the workaholic part of Luke wouldn't suspect they were really having fun.

They set a crab pot off the end of the dock at the boat basin and caught a succulent dinner. They scrambled over sharp rocks, at low tide in a drizzling rain, and gathered blue-black mussels from exposed rocks. Luke hadn't even known this shellfish was edible, but Cindy turned them into a delectable delicacy, rich with fragrant garlic butter.

They visited a cheese factory, where a friend of Cindy's took them behind the scenes and showed them cheese making in process. At the end of the tour the friend presented them with a sack of cheese curds. Luke expected something blah and slimy, but the cheese curds turned out to be rounded, irregular chunks of mild cheddar that had an unexpectedly squeaky texture when eaten.

They gathered interesting bits of shell and driftwood, some of which Cindy turned into a comical little trio of fantasy sea creatures huddled in the bowl of a clam shell. She sold the creation the very next day at the kite shop. The next one he refused to let her sell and kept for himself, smiling every time he looked at the sad-funny little creatures of shell and bark peering up at him from his coffee table.

But when he saw Cindy eyeing a recipe in the local newspaper, the main ingredients of which appeared to be seaweed and squid, he drew the line.

"It is time," he announced, "for fun of a less...mmm...self-sufficient variety. Time for something that normal people do for fun."

She looked up from the newspaper. They were at her place, having just finished bowls of homemade clam chowder. "Such as?"

"Dinner out. Dinner that we haven't captured, so to speak, on the hoof. Dinner with a hovering waiter, champagne and something sinfully delicious for dessert. Followed by music and dancing. I thought we might drive up to Portland."

Luke half expected Cindy to object, to flutter in agitation that she was a small-town girl who hadn't the proper clothes for a night out in the big city. But she just gave him a lazy-lidded look and a sunny smile. "Sounds good to me."

LUKE SWALLOWED HARD when he saw Cindy that Saturday evening. He hadn't expected her to be in her usual costume of jeans and shirt, but neither was he quite prepared for the vision that greeted him, a totally unexpected blend of fragile sophistication and sexy loveliness. Her dress, with a ladylike front ruffle, was a demure pale amethyst, its color echoing the delicacy of her pale-blond hair and honey-tinted skin. Her silvery-amethyst fingernail polish matched the dress. Her hair was done in a sleek upswirl.

But the cut of the dress was not demure. The back was deliciously bare, and when she moved the skirt had a flirty swing and the front ruffle parted to reveal a tantalizing glimpse of curved bosom. A single tendril of long hair hung down her bare back, almost inviting a man to brush it aside and kiss the smooth skin.

Cindy was less surprised but no less impressed with Luke's appearance in a classically cut charcoal suit, silver and black diagonally striped silk tie . . . and a look in his eyes that sent her heart dancing like a kite on a skittish wind.

He took both her hands in his. "I like," he stated, the compliment somehow all the more flattering for its bluntness.

"Like what?"

He put a hand on her shoulder and spun her in front of him until the flaring skirt caught on his legs. "Everything." He ended the spin by drawing her into his arms. Her back was to him, his arms around her waist. His lips nuzzled her ear. "I like everything about you. The way you look. The way you smell. The way you feel."

The spin made her feel delightfully giddy. She wondered why she didn't dress up more often. She hadn't worn this dress since she'd bought it for a New Year's Eve party over a year ago. She loved feeling all frothy and feminine, especially when she was pressed against the lean length of this man's body. She turned around, then stepped back and let her gaze travel down his impressive figure before rising to catch the gleam in the rich, dark depths of his eyes. "I like everything, too." In fact, she thought a little tremulously, maybe she much more than liked. . . .

"We'd better go," Luke said. "If we don't . . ." He left the sentence unfinished, but his meaning and his faint smile were temptingly clear.

The drive to Portland took almost two hours, but the giddy feeling that had come with the breathless spin into Luke's arms didn't go away. They sang duets with Willy Nelson and Julio Iglesias on the radio, talked back to callers on a talk show, and counted out-of-state license plates, their spirits undampened by the rainy weather.

If anything, Cindy's giddy feeling increased as the evening progressed. They had dinner at one of Portland's most elegant restaurants, a place she'd heard of but had never been to. They chose food that had never been near the sea and finished with a spectacular flaming dessert.

When the lounge where they were dancing closed at two a.m., they went to an all-night restaurant for coffee.

Then something happened to dampen the giddiness and dump her back into reality. A couple Cindy knew from Steller Beach passed their booth, saw her and stopped in surprise. There were introductions and flurries of "Imagine seeing you here!" The couple had come to Portland to celebrate their anniversary and were making a night of it. They were an outgoing, friendly pair and obviously expected to be invited to join Luke and Cindy. Reluctantly Cindy made the gesture, and they accepted.

Her uneasiness came because she was uncertain of Luke's reaction. He'd never actually avoided her friends. Joanna had reported that she'd had a pleasant conversation with him one day when he'd come into the kite shop while Cindy was out. But she'd never forgotten his wary statement about not getting involved with people and that he'd been only polite, not friendly, to Cece at the Chowder House. He'd apparently relaxed that noninvolvement rule with regard to Cindy, but their activities had never included more than just the two of them, and she suspected the exclusion of outsiders was not accidental.

However, to her surprise, Luke was more than cordial to the Brentons. He wasn't *overly* friendly, of course, but his mood was genial, and he didn't seem to resent the intrusion.

The two couples wound up sitting and talking over coffee until past four o'clock in the morning.

Even at that late—or early—hour, Cindy's exhilaration didn't droop. She felt like talking, laughing, singing her happiness, high not on the champagne she'd had with dinner hours before but on a buoyant feeling that she strongly suspected could be labeled falling in love.

On the drive home Luke suggested she get some sleep, but she answered gaily, "Who wants to waste a marvelous night such as this on sleep?"

Perhaps if she could have snuggled up to him she would have fallen asleep, content with the feel of her head on his shoulder, but the bucket seats prevented that. So she wanted to stay awake to savor all the other marvelous messages that her senses brought to her about him: the sound of his voice and laugh, the sight of his strong profile in the dim light from the dashboard, the scent of an outdoorsy after-shave that blended with a fresh dampness that clung to his clothing after their dash from restaurant to car.

"Don't forget you have to work tomorrow," he reminded her. "Actually by now it's today."

Cindy had arranged with Joanna and another part-time salesclerk, Sue, for them to handle the kite shop on Sunday. But just before Cindy and Luke had left for Portland on Saturday evening, Sue had called and apologetically said her little boy was sick and she wouldn't be able to make it.

Even the thought of work in just a few hours didn't dampen Cindy's spirits. At the moment she felt as if she might never need sleep again.

Yet just a few miles outside Steller Beach, drowsiness did overtake her. She couldn't put her head on Luke's shoulder, so she curled her hand around his thigh as she drifted off. His hand covered hers companionably.

But before she was quite asleep she made a decision. Luke had made progress, no doubt about it. They'd had a marvelous evening of light-hearted fun, and he'd accepted the intrusion of back-home acquaintances with equanimity. Yes, he was ready for something more, ready to be gently gathered into the circle of her friends, ready to get involved with people again.

But when her eyes drifted open, when she was awakened by the feel of strong arms lifting her out of the car in a rain-washed dawn, she realized Luke had immediate plans of his own in mind. . . plans that definitely included only the two of them.

5

CINDY THOUGHT ABOUT SAYING she could walk, but she didn't. She just closed her eyes again and curled her face into Luke's chest, drifting with the delightful sensation of being carried in strong, protective arms. He'd apparently already unlocked the cottage, because he nudged the door open with his knee.

He carried her directly to the bedroom. She felt herself being lowered to the bed, the pillow adjusted beneath her head.

"Cindy?" he whispered. His hand rested lightly on her stomach, and a palm print of warmth seeped through the silky fabric. "Are you awake?"

She murmured something unintelligible, her mind too drifty and dreamy to form real words. For a moment his hands went away, and she was about to open one eye to see why, but then he turned her gently on her side. The movement brought her a notch closer to full awakening, and she realized he was trying to figure out how the backless dress was fastened.

She supposed she should help him, but the feeling of his hands moving over her, searching at her waist and fumbling with the hidden zipper, was too sweet to interrupt. She let herself go limp as he slid the ruffled top of the dress over her breasts, hoping a firming of nipples at his touch didn't give away her awareness. He lifted her body in order to lower the dress over her waist, giving her hips a tantalizing upward tilt.

She was fully awake by then, tinglingly aware of each sensation, and yet she had the strange feeling that she was dreaming, too, that the touch of his fingertips and glide of his palms across hips and stomach was too magical to be real. He paused while removing the dress to slip off her shoes, and never had she known that feathery touches on her feet could be so erotic. After shoes and dress came panty hose, and she shivered lightly with the pleasure of his touch on inner thighs and knees and ankles.

When she was finally lying there in nothing but the lacy bits of her underwear, she felt him looking down at her. She could hear his breathing, too, a little too rough and rapid to be caused merely by the physical exertion involved in undressing her.

She thought he'd remove her underwear next, but instead he again slid an arm beneath her so that he could lift her lightly. He pulled out the covers and spread them over her. Then there was silence, and she waited breathlessly for the sound of his clothes being removed and the weight of his body sagging the other side of the single bed.

When she neither heard nor felt anything, she cautiously opened one eye. The bedroom door was just closing behind him, only his fingers visible as he tried to ease it shut without waking her.

"Luke!" she cried, her pretense of being asleep forgotten.

The door opened again, and he peered around it.

"I'm sorry. I didn't mean to wake you."

"Where are you going?"

"Out to the kitchen to make coffee."

"But I thought...I mean..." When he merely looked mildly perplexed at her stammered words, she put her thoughts more bluntly. "Aren't you coming to bed, too?"

"I'm not sleepy."

"That isn't exactly what I meant."

"It's only a couple of hours until you have to get up and go to work. You can't play all night and work all day without a little sleep in between. And you, sweet Cinnamon, refused to go to sleep on the drive home." He smiled benignly.

"I don't need sleep," she argued heatedly. She tossed back the covers, not thinking whether she did so in defiance or invitation. "I'd much rather—"

"Make love?" he filled in helpfully.

She didn't bother to deny it.

He returned to the bed, but when he reached for her he merely tucked the covers around her again, his touch solicitous rather than seductive. "Remember what I told you once?"

She remembered a number of things, but none that seemed relevant at that particular moment.

"I told you that when we make love, it isn't going to be under a time limit, when there's a getting-to-work deadline to meet."

"But—but it was different then!" That was before she ached with wanting him, before she fell in love with him. "And you don't have to go to work!"

"But you do, and a time limit is a time limit," he stated with a firm logic that frustrated her. "I shouldn't have kept you out so late. When I make love to you . . ." He drew his fingertips down her cheek and across her lips, leaving a trail that felt incandescent, giving her a sweet taste of what might have been. He smiled in a way that made her feel weak from throat to toes. "I want all the time in the world."

"But I don't need sleep," she protested weakly. "Honestly I don't. And it's a long time until morning." A sliver of morning sunshine peeping through a crack in the draperies belied that argument.

"Sweet dreams, sweet Cinnamon." He made a singsong little rhyme of the words as he tucked the covers more tightly around her shoulders. "I'll have breakfast ready and wake you in time to get to work."

He closed the door softly behind him.

Cindy's thoughts momentarily raged at him for being so stubborn, at herself for not realizing the consequences of her blithe desire to dance the night away and then refusing to sleep on the drive home. But she was smiling when she slipped into sleep only moments later. Infuriating man...sweet man...man she was tumbling helplessly in love with.

HE'D BEEN to the downtown coffee shop and bakery by the time he wakened her. The tray he brought to her bed held warm croissants and apricot preserves, icy orange juice and steaming coffee.

"I think I'm dreaming," Cindy murmured as he arranged pillows behind her so she could sit up and eat.

He perched on the edge of the bed and shared the breakfast with her.

"Dreaming about me?" he asked.

"You don't deserve to be dreamed about," she muttered.

He just laughed and didn't ask for an explanation.

CINDY CONSIDERED AND REJECTED several plans for introducing Luke to a social life with her friends. She wanted him to see that the world was full of good people, nice people, if you just gave them a chance. She considered having a few couples over for dinner at her place, but decided that would be too crowded. And people might wind up just sitting around and talking, and perhaps innocently asking questions that would make Luke freeze. Party? She could talk Joanna into giving one at her rambling old house. No. A good party would include too many people, and Luke could deftly avoid involvement with individuals.

She finally decided on a beach barbecue, something breezy and casual. Conversation wouldn't tend to get personal, and there would be things to do: gathering driftwood for a fire, roasting wieners and marshmallows, maybe playing volleyball or touch football. Three other couples besides Luke and her, she decided. Enough to make a lively group but not enough to overwhelm him.

The only problem was picking a suitable day when everyone could come. Luke's days off suddenly got changed to Monday and Tuesday, which helped. She then invited friends mostly on the basis of who was available on a weekday afternoon. Joanna and Max, of course. Louise and Dan Denton, a slightly older couple who owned the ice cream shop next to the kite store, which was also closed Mondays. And Pam Dubuque and Kylie Anderson, who had been part of her team at the sand castle contest the previous year.

She had everything set before she told Luke. She was half afraid he might make some flimsy excuse not to come or perhaps not bother with excuses and simply give her a flat no.

Instead, apparently remembering some of their previous activities, he was more suspicious of the food than the people. "I'm almost afraid to ask what it is we're going to barbecue."

"Dogs."

He considered that. "I presume you *are* talking about the ordinary supermarket variety of hot dogs?"

She grinned. "Of course."

He grinned back, nodded agreement, and the impact of that smile on her heart made Cindy wonder wryly if she wasn't making a big mistake exposing him to people, some of them female. Pam was an old friend, vivacious and fun, but she was also known for her flirty ways. Kylie and Pam were living together, not married. If she was smart, she concluded with a sigh, she should probably just hide Luke away and keep him all to herself.

Luke then asked who was coming to the barbecue. Cindy named the guests. Luke didn't appear wildly enthusiastic, but he didn't back out.

Plans went smoothly. Joanna's husband rounded up a volleyball net and beach chairs. Louise volunteered to bring soft drinks; Pam and Kylie offered beer. Cindy selected and bought the food. Luke insisted on paying for half.

Everything went fine until Sunday evening. Joanna called. She was difficult to hear because of all the noise in the background.

"Cindy, I have a problem." Shriek and clunk.

"Don't tell me you can't come tomorrow!"

"Oh, we can come. It's just that my brother-in-law and his wife and kids just showed up to spend a few days with us. I wasn't expecting them until next week. He's looking for a job here." Yelp and crash. "Would it be all right if they come, too?"

Cindy hesitated. She wanted Luke to get involved with people; she thought he was ready. But she hadn't planned to expose him to children just yet. That might be too much too soon.

"Don't the children have to go to school? Tomorrow is a school day."

"Well, they've just arrived, and they don't know if they're going to stay, so the kids aren't enrolled yet."

"Oh. Of course." Cindy searched for some other polite excuse. "The kids probably wouldn't have much fun. There won't be any other children there."

"I don't think they need any other children to have fun. There are five of them." Joanna sounded a little harried.

"Five!" Cindy echoed.

Thunderous woofing. "And a dog. A very big dog. I really would like to take them some place where they could work off a little steam." Now Joanna sounded a bit desperate. "They've been cooped up in a car for two days."

There wasn't much Cindy could do but give in gracefully and hope for the best. Five kids. One dog. One voluptuous-bodied brunette with roving eyes. A weather report that said an offshore storm was headed inland. It was all beginning to sound like a recipe for disaster. Gloomily she made another trip downtown and bought more wieners, buns and another big can of pork and beans.

THE DAY DIDN'T START too badly, however. Cindy and Luke arrived first. The size of the waves on the retreating tide hinted at a storm out there somewhere, but so far it was no more than a dark bank of clouds on the horizon. Here bright sunlight reflected off Luke's mirrored sunglasses, and a frisky breeze whirled the camp fire flames in a merry dance.

Joanna, Max and relatives arrived next. Kids and dog exploded out of the two cars. Cindy thought there were two girls and three boys, although they careered around so energetically that she couldn't be certain. And was there really just *one* dog? He seemed to be everywhere. Dragging a wet stick out of the surf, snitching a wiener, indiscriminately showering everyone with a shake of seawater from his heavy black fur. And all the time grinning with such disarming cheerfulness that he couldn't be maligned. He took a special liking to Luke and presented him with an assortment of salvaged treasures: a slithery strand of seaweed, a rotten stick, a crumpled beer can.

Max set up the volleyball net, and they started a game when the other couples arrived. Cindy kept sneaking glances at Luke, wondering what he thought of all this, wondering if he was going to manage to hit the ball with Pam waving her little bikini-clad bottom in front of him. Everyone else was in jeans or shorts, but not Pam.

With the mirrored sunglasses hiding his eyes, it was more difficult than ever to tell what he was thinking. But by the time everyone had eaten and had draped themselves in various well-fed poses around the camp fire, Cindy was aware that he was acting differently than when the two of them were alone. He wasn't unfriendly. On the surface he fitted comfortably with the group. He kept up his end of the male conversation about sports, mill work and the local economy.

But she could sense that old barrier of reserve, as if he was on guard. She could tell that he carefully chose his answers to the few stray personal questions that came his way.

Then Pam plopped down in front of him, squirming her bottom into the sand as she sat in cross-legged fashion. "I understand that you're from Massachusetts," she said brightly. Joanna must have mentioned that to Pam; Cindy knew *she* hadn't. "My brother Clark lives back there."

"Oh?" Polite but wary. And definitely not an encouragement to continue.

Pam apparently didn't get the message. "In Brookline. I think it's near Boston."

For all the reaction he showed, Luke might never have heard of either place, in spite of the fact that he'd lived in Boston.

"Clark's a stockbroker."

If Cindy hadn't been so surprised, she might have laughed. She could almost—but not quite, of course—feel sorry for Pam, because she knew instinctively that with that innocent statement Pam had just killed any chances she might have had to add Luke to her list of conquests. Cindy could tell it from the way Luke straightened in the lounge chair, one hand tensed around the metal armrest.

His reaction gave her a moment's uneasy pause. Just because he had decided to leave Boston and get out of stocks and bonds hardly seemed sufficient reason to treat Pam with such icy hostility. Pam was, after all, just a harmless flirt. Cindy suddenly wondered—not for the first time—if there was more to his past than he'd told her. It occurred to her that he hadn't worn those sunglasses by accident. They were a subtle way of shutting people out, of affirming that invisible but almost impenetrable wall he had erected between himself and people in general.

After a few more unsuccessful attempts at making conversation with Luke, Pam flounced back to Kylie, where her flirty talents were more appreciated.

The kids were first to revive after eating, of course. They started a game of tag, dog included. One of the little girls fascinated Cindy. She was about eight, not the youngest of the children but certainly the smallest. She was a natural daredevil, escaping a tag by darting up a rock too steep for the others to climb, blithely leaping off the far side. In spite of her small size, she was so quick that she could taunt the larger children by mischievously letting them get almost close enough to tag her, then darting away. And her methods of escape were often unique. She was as apt to turn a cartwheel or flip as she was to twist and turn on her feet.

"Has your little girl had gymnastic training?" Cindy asked her mother, Melanie.

Melanie glanced at her daughter, who was just then catapulting off a driftwood log. "Tracy? No. I thought about sending her to some classes at a gymnastics school back home, but I never got around to it."

"She has a lot of natural talent."

Melanie laughed. "Sometimes I call it something else when I catch her standing on her hands on a banister or vaulting over the living-room furniture."

One of the children raced back to ask Cindy if she'd brought along a kite. She hadn't, but she created one out of a paper plate, a couple of drinking straws, with a tail made of Styrofoam cups, the odd assortment of parts strung together with some old kite string she had in the pickup.

Luke turned the lounge chair so that he could watch. Cindy looked hardly older than the children she was playing with, he mused as he watched her race down the beach, hair flying, to get the makeshift kite aloft. But she'd been all woman when he put her to bed the other night. He'd mentally kicked himself a few times for insisting on holding out for a no-time-limit occasion. He'd thought at the time that the proper occasion would come almost immediately, but for various frustrating reasons, bad luck and poor timing, it hadn't.

"Great gal," Dan offered. "She's done wonders with that kite shop."

Luke remembered then that Cindy had said Dan and Louise had the ice cream store next to the kite shop. They were a little older than the other couples.

Dan laughed. "Would you believe she even talked me into buying one of those big box kites? She told me it would get my mind off my troubles, and it does. When you're flying one of those in a high wind, you don't have time to think about anything else."

"I suppose it could be fun, if you like that sort of thing. I guess I'm just too practical." Cindy had the kite up now. She handed the string to one of the boys. "I keep seeing all that wind energy going to waste and thinking it ought to be useful for something more important then flying kites."

"Well, it may be. I hear there's a new company coming in that's going to build one of those big wind farms like they have down in California. They use a kind of modernized windmill to produce electricity from wind power."

"Wind turbines they're called," Luke offered, recalling the information from a company he'd investigated when he was with the Marianna Funds. "Of course it takes a number of wind turbines to produce electricity on a commercial scale, but it's a fascinating alternative to the more conventional energy sources."

"Yes, it is. And no pollution. Oh-oh, there goes the kite."

A freak gust of wind zoomed the kite to just a few feet above ground level, and Howser, the dog, made a gleeful lunge at it. End of kite.

Cindy returned, winding the kite string around a stick as she came. "Well, that didn't last long." She laughed.

"But it was pretty clever." Luke admired self-sufficiency even when it dealt only with kite flying. "I guess I'd never realized a paper plate could be made to fly as a kite."

"Almost anything can be made to fly. I heard a story once about a disgruntled storekeeper who pieced together all the bad checks his store had received and flew them. And I've heard about a bikini that was sent aloft. Of course, it was too small to fly very well." She threw a look at Pam, who was making a production number out of spreading a towel on the sand.

Luke just laughed and pulled her across his lap in the chair and kissed her, not caring who was watching. Pam's boldly exposed body had nothing on the tantalizing figure he'd seen in the pale blue lingerie the other night. And the shallowness of Pam's ways could never tempt him to stray from Cindy. He had to keep reminding himself that it wouldn't be fair to fall in love with her.

THEY SAT AROUND THE FIRE a while longer. Then Dan's wife, Louise, who had been napping in a lounge chair nearby, stood up and stretched. "Anyone want to wander up to the rest rooms in the park with me?"

Cindy, Joanna and Melanie decided to go along. Pam shook her head. The kids had already been up to the rest rooms numerous times, of course. They were now constructing a fort in the driftwood.

"Watch the kids, will you, hon?" Melanie called to her husband. He nodded without looking at either her or the children. Pam had just decided to dazzle him with the undivided-attention treatment, and he was a little glassy-eyed.

"Does that...uh...bother you?" Cindy asked, not wanting any unpleasantness to arise.

Melanie looked mildly puzzled, then realized Cindy was referring to Pam's antics. She laughed. "I'm sure Mike could use a little ego boosting from the attentions of a pretty girl. Then he'll come swaggering back to me with his batteries all recharged." She looked as unruffled as she sounded.

Definitely an attitude to aim for, Cindy thought to herself.

They went to the rest rooms, then wandered over to look at some azalea and rhododendron bushes that interested Melanie. From this point, Cindy couldn't see the camp fire or the kids, but she could see Pam and Kylie walking arm in arm down the beach. Apparently the battery recharging was over.

The other women decided to stroll downtown, but Cindy headed back to the beach. On the way she met the three husbands. They'd decided to try surf fishing and were going back to Max's to pick up equipment.

"But . . . but that means Luke is alone with the kids."

The father of said children managed an injured look. "They're just children, not pint-sized terrorists. Luke is safe with them. I told them to stay away from the water. Melanie should be back in a minute."

Cindy didn't pause to argue about how soon Melanie might return. She just raced down the beach, berating herself for having stayed away so long. Luke would be furious at having gotten stuck with a baby-sitting job. She'd never get him to another social outing. She'd be lucky if he would even speak to her after this.

Then she realized that the beach chairs were deserted, the camp fire burned to embers. Where *was* Luke? Anger and worry about the children replaced her apprehension. Even if he resented the unwanted responsibility, he had no right just to walk out on them!

Then she heard sounds from where the children had been building their fort in the driftwood. She raced over and scrambled up the rough side of a huge log. Only two children and the dog were in sight. She tried not to panic. "Where is everybody?"

"We're in here," a deep voice responded from within a pile of driftwood that she now realized was a makeshift shelter. On hands and knees, Luke peered around an upright slab of driftwood. His sunglasses were pushed back and tangled in his rumpled hair. A small boy's face bobbed around beside him.

"Luke, what are you *doing*?" She jumped off the log.

"The kids were having a problem with the roof. I'm supplying architectural and engineering advice. We could use a little help with the manual labour." His shirt was draped over a nearby log, and his bare chest looked even harder and more muscular than she remembered from the massage she'd once given him. He was perspiring lightly, and silky whorls of hair clung to his damp, gleaming skin.

"You're not . . . angry?"

"Well, I was pretty discouraged when the roof started to cave in," he answered seriously, "but we have it braced now."

The little daredevil, Tracy, drew a strand of long hair across her upper lip as if trying to hide her face. The blond mustache only made her look even more mischievous. She squirmed a bare toe in the sand. "I guess it was my fault. I was climbing on top."

Luke came out of the shelter and stood up. "Okay, you kids, we gotta get this thing going. The Vikings may attack any minute. Joe, find some rocks to stack around the corner posts. Tracy and Lisa, look for flat pieces of bark to rebuild the roof. Todd and Bobby, start digging a moat. Blond lady, you help me carry this big chunk of driftwood."

The children jumped to their tasks, and Cindy was too surprised to do anything but comply, as well. She was surprised, first that he wasn't furious at being left alone with the kids. Surprised next that he was playing with them. And further surprised that he knew their names and which name belonged to which child. She'd got only one name definitely so far. Tracy's.

The roof was rebuilt of poles and bark, a moat dug and small logs were arranged into a protective wall. The tide was heading in now, but it was still a long way from the moat. When all was complete, Luke sent out two spies. They returned with the information that no Vikings were in sight, but there were fishermen who were telling tales of huge sea creatures.

"My daddy says one fish was this big!" Tracy stretched her arms to full length.

"The ones that get away are always that big," an older boy said wisely. "The ones that get caught are this big." He measured a minuscule space with his fingers.

"I wonder why that is," Cindy murmured.

"My daddy lets those big ones go," Tracy confided. "He says they won't fit in the pan, anyway." For no apparent reason other than that she was filled with exuberant energy, she turned a back flip and followed it with a cartwheel.

"Can you do a one-armed cartwheel?" Cindy asked.

"Sure." The little girl did two for good measure.

"How about an aerial cartwheel?" Cindy asked. She was intrigued by what the little girl could do without ever having had any training.

"What's that?"

"It's a cartwheel without your hands touching the ground." Cindy was almost tempted to show Tracy how to do it, until she realized Luke was looking at her rather oddly. "Hey, I think it's time to eat again. I'm hungry. How about the rest of you?"

They trooped back to the fire. The sun had already slipped into the offshore bank of clouds that was perceptibly closer and darker now. Even hot-blooded Pam had been forced to cover up in the cooler air.

The last of the food disappeared under this second onslaught of hungry appetites. Everyone sat around the camp fire until the sky overhead was divided into two halves, the inland half still clear and starry, the seaward portion blotted with clouds. Luke seemed more relaxed now, less wary. Kylie was working on the reforestation project that Luke had wanted to join, and they had a lot to talk about.

Louise and Dan were the first to leave, then Joanna, Max and their relatives. Kylie and Pam had been snuggling together in a lounge chair. When Max cheerfully dumped them out as he was gathering up chairs, Pam produced a blanket from somewhere, and they simply moved to a sheltered hollow by a log near the camp fire. They lay facing the fire, bodies spooned together.

With the children gone, the night sea sounds seemed suddenly louder and stronger. No moonlight filtered through the clouds that were rapidly consuming the shrinking stretch of starry sky, but Cindy could tell the high-tide waves weren't far beyond the flicker of camp fire light. The beach appeared deserted apart from another fire to the south.

"Are you ready to leave?" Cindy asked Luke.

"Not yet. It's . . . mmm . . . rather peaceful here now."

"Now that the rug rats are gone," Kylie said.

Pam twisted around and punched his shoulder. "That's no way to talk about kids. Someday we're going to have—"

"Less than five," Kylie cut in with a laugh. This time Pam gave him a bump with her bottom, which Cindy suspected was not exactly a heartless punishment. "Maybe two," he conceded.

Cindy and Luke were sitting cross-legged by the fire, knees touching, but in nowhere near as intimate a position as the other couple. Cindy didn't know whether to feel embarrassed or envious about the display. She suspected Pam and Kylie thought she and Luke were on closer terms than was actually the case, so she quickly headed the conversation in a different direction before Pam could start inquiring about their family-making plans. Modesty and tact were not Pam's strong points.

"What about this year's sand castle contest?" Cindy asked. "Are we going to get a team together again?"

"We lost our construction engineer when Doug moved away," Kylie reminded her. "Without a supervisor to pull our efforts together, our castle might wind up looking like a glorified outhouse."

"Steller Beach has a big sand sculpture festival every year," Cindy explained to Luke. "Last year we did this sand castle being attacked by a two-headed dragon."

Pam giggled. "Except it had only one head, because the other one fell off before the judging."

"We didn't win anything," Cindy admitted to Luke.

"We never win anything," Kylie said complacently. "But we have a hell of a lot of fun."

Pam and Kylie left a few minutes later. Pam slyly willed the old blanket to them, whispering reminiscently to Cindy. "I remember the first time Kylie and I made love on the beach. . . ."

Cindy began to say coolly, "Thanks, Pam, but—"

But Luke was already claiming the blanket, as if he'd had an envious eye on it all along. When Pam and Kylie were gone he stretched out on it and held out his arms to Cindy.

"C'mon, that wind is getting cold. We'll stay just until the fire dies down again."

Cindy had no intention of letting what Pam had just suggested actually happen. Making love on the beach, indeed! She wasn't quite that uninhibited. She rationalized her decision to join Luke on the blanket with the self-righteous thought that the wind definitely was getting brisker and chillier.

But the little shiver that tingled through her had nothing to do with the strength or chill of the wind.

6

LUKE SNUGGLED HER into the curve of his body, her back to his chest, his own back protected by the log. He rearranged sand beneath the blanket into a pillow for her head, then drew her hair aside and kissed her lightly on the back of the neck.

"Isn't this better than sitting over there in the wind?" he whispered.

"Much."

The camp fire flickered and danced, the smoky scent mingling with smells of sea and coming rain. The crash of waves on the incoming tide moved ever closer, but the sound was not an intrusion. It enveloped them in an intimate world of their own, hung a curtain of sound around this island of firelight. They lay facing the fire, his arm tucked around her waist, the silence between them companionable yet laced with powerful undercurrents of a deeper man/woman awareness.

Luke reached behind him to bring the blanket up over them. When his arm returned to enclose her, his hand found her breast and cupped it gently. The touch was as companionable as the silence, as erotic as the undercurrents. She rubbed the bare sole of her foot over the solid instep of his, savoring the feel.

"Did you have fun today?" he asked.

"Of course. But . . . did you?"

"You sound as if you don't think I did."

She hesitated a moment and then chose honesty. "Except when you were with the kids, I had the feeling you were. . .filtering almost every word you said through a screen of caution. As if you suspected the answers might someday be hurled back at you in a cross-examination."

"Odd that you should phrase it just that way."

For a moment she thought the bluntness of her comment had angered him. Then she realized, as she glanced back over her shoulder, that he was more pensive than angry.

"I was really surprised to find you helping the kids build their fort," she admitted. "Pleasantly surprised."

"Why? You thought I didn't like children?"

"You seem to have rather strong reservations about just liking *people*, and kids can sometimes be rather noisy, exuberant little people."

"I like kids. I haven't been around them much, but I don't mind their noise or energy. Kids are real, not phony. You can trust them." Luke's unexpected vehemence surprised Cindy. "You don't have to wonder if they're out to get you or plotting behind your back or turning what you say into some incriminating evidence against you."

"Someone did that to you, didn't they? When you were with the mutual funds company?" She had always suspected there was more to his departure from that high-powered world than he'd told her.

"Several someones, actually."

Cindy waited, uncertain whether to probe or lead him into telling her more. She felt such an upsurge of love for him, such a fierce protectiveness combined with fury at those unknown someones who had harmed him and made him so bitter. She turned to face him, her head on the pillow of sand, and locked her hands behind his neck.

"Tell me," she said simply.

"Perhaps you'll feel differently about me once you know."

"I love you." She hadn't intended to say the words so soon. They hadn't, until that moment, even been clearly formed in her mind, although the emotion was there. She supposed she had hoped he would say them first. But she wasn't sorry she'd said them, and she repeated them fiercely. "I love you."

He didn't disregard the statement, but seemed to set it aside, to place it on hold so that she could snatch it back if she chose. "Some people think I'm an embezzler."

Cindy raised herself on one elbow. She didn't know what she'd expected, perhaps a revelation of some vicious infighting for power within the company, ruthless competition for a promotion, something like that. She looked into his dark eyes, grave in spite of the reflection of dancing firelight in their depths. She was shocked by what he'd said, yet certain of her reaction.

"That's ridiculous. You're not an embezzler!"

"What makes you so positive?"

"Because . . . because you're too honest. The very first day we met, you wound up with a few dollars too much change on our bed purchase, and you insisted on recalculating until every penny was right."

"A man might be honest about a few dollars but dishonest if the stakes were much larger, say in the thousands of dollars," he pointed out.

"I told you that day that I trusted you—"

"I remember."

"And I still trust you."

She put her head back on the blanket and pulled him close so that only a few inches separated their eyes. He drew her fingertips to his lips and kissed them. She threw one leg over his to hold his body close, her heel digging into the calf of his leg as she waited for him to go on.

"An audit, commissioned by management above me, revealed almost a hundred thousand dollars missing from the Marianna Energy Fund," he began, reluctantly but steadily. "It was a complicated scheme that involved juggling figures in the computer among a number of individual accounts to avoid detection. Apparently it had been going on for some time before the irregularities were suspected, and the higher echelons of management didn't trust anyone. I didn't even know the audit was scheduled until it began. The shortage in funds was traced to me."

"But how could it have been when you didn't do it!"

"That's what I kept asking myself. But so help me, that's the way it looked." He shook his head as if that fact still dazed him. Wryly he added, "If I hadn't known I was innocent, I would probably have believed I was guilty, too."

"Then what happened?"

"I was arrested but released on bail. I was suspended from my job, which, under the circumstances, was quite proper, of course. I felt angry and frustrated, but I was certain everything would be cleared up quickly and my innocence proven beyond doubt."

"And?"

"The accused shall have the right to a fair and speedy trial, right? The accused is innocent until proven guilty, correct?" Luke answered the sardonic questions himself. "Not necessarily. The thing dragged on and on. The prosecution would make one move; my lawyer would counter it with another. I felt like a pawn, trapped in a chess game of complicated legal maneuvers. I thought a different audit would surely prove my innocence, and I personally paid to have one conducted."

"What did it show?"

"Practically the same thing as the first one. Whoever took the money was very, very clever. A damn sight more clever with a computer than I am, in fact—although no one else seemed to believe that."

"Your lawyer believed in your innocence, didn't he?"

"If he did, he was practically the only one. I had the impression he was more concerned about his professional reputation than with my guilt or innocence."

"But surely friends, people who really knew you, couldn't believe you were guilty?"

"Couldn't they?" His laugh was short and bitter. "I didn't think so, either, and at first I did receive some tentative support. But people didn't exactly rally 'round. Very quickly I realized my so-called friends thought any show of support for me could threaten their own positions in the company. They figured association with me might also blacken them. And they were probably right. I imagine a few of them also began to see opportunity in the situation. If I was out as assistant manager, perhaps one of them would be in. It soon became expedient to dissociate oneself from any connection with me."

"But that doesn't mean they actually thought you were guilty."

"The result was the same."

Yes, it probably was, Cindy realized regretfully. Now she was beginning to understand that wall of reserve he'd built around himself, his wariness about involvement with people. He'd been burned, and he wasn't about to let it happen again.

"But friends from outside the company—"

"I was a workaholic, remember? My 'friends' were business associates or acquaintances. And the suspicion wasn't all one-sided, of course, because I knew—and I still know—that someone out there was guilty of what I was accused of. Maybe it's someone I thought of as a friend. If I wasn't deliberately framed, someone at least let me take the blame for his guilt. And perhaps I *was* deliberately framed. I suppose I've stepped on a few toes over the years. Or maybe I was just chosen at random. In any case, the result was, again, the same."

"But when the trial was held and you were found innocent— You *were* found innocent, weren't you?" Cindy asked, shaken by a sudden, sinking feeling that perhaps justice hadn't been done.

"Yes, I was found innocent. Technically, anyway."

"What do you mean?"

"My lawyer found some irregularities in the gathering of the evidence. He managed to get much of it thrown out so it couldn't be used against me at the trial. Without it, the case fell apart, and the jury found me innocent. But not before the prosecution put some of my former friends and co-workers on the stand, and statements I'd made and actions I'd taken in the past were twisted and used against me."

"Oh, Luke, I'm so—so sorry."

"The whole thing also wiped me out financially, of course. Legal fees, investigative fees, the expense of the audit . . . you wouldn't believe how much it can cost under our legal system for an innocent man to prove his innocence. And it didn't do a hell of a lot of good."

"Why do you say that?"

"The company reinstated me in my job. I didn't realize at the time how reluctant they were to do so, that they did it only on the advice of their own lawyers, in fact. And I accepted. But it took only a short time to make me realize that although the trial may have cleared me legally, it hadn't cleared me in people's minds. If anything, it had damned me. The general opinion was that I was as guilty as a thief caught with a hand in the cash register, and a smart lawyer had simply gotten me off on a legal technicality. I realized I couldn't stay on where no one trusted me, where I was really on probation trying to prove my innocence and every move I made was under a shadow of suspicion."

"Surely the real thief will be caught before long."

"Maybe. The disappearance of funds stopped when I was suspended from my job, of course."

"But people must realize that doesn't mean anything! The embezzler wouldn't be dumb enough to continue his activities, or it would be obvious you weren't guilty."

Luke shrugged. "The whole thing disillusioned me about friendships, soured me on trusting people and jaundiced my view of both the corporate and legal systems. It also eliminated any future for me in the field of work I was good at, cared about and enjoyed."

"Luke, I realize how terrible this has been for you. But there are lots of good, loyal people who stand by their friends in time of trouble. You don't have to be so on guard with people like those who were here today."

"As I've said, I just figure it's better not to get too involved."

Cindy wanted to ask if that included herself, but suddenly she was afraid to push the issue. She might just drive him away if she asked for too much too soon. His face had a darkly brooding expression in the faint glow from the dying fire.

Instead she said, "And in spite of your jaundiced feeling about the legal system, it did work, albeit a bit haphazardly. You were found innocent."

"Perhaps only because I had the money to pay for a smart and very expensive lawyer." He laughed harshly. "The joke going around was that the reason I could hire such a good lawyer was because I had all that embezzled money to pay him with."

Cindy swallowed. This wasn't going very well. She made one more effort. "Your future in the stock market or in mutual funds isn't necessarily ended. After all, you were found innocent. And we're on the opposite side of the country from where it happened. You could make a fresh start here."

"News like that gets around. Sometimes people remember the accusation better than the outcome of a trial."

Cindy raised herself on one elbow again. She looked hard at him for a long moment. Then she grabbed his ear, not gently. "Luke Townsend, you snap out of it," she commanded. She tugged at his ear so hard that his whole head shook. "Look on the bright side of things for a change. You're young and healthy. You have a perfectly good job at the mill. You have people who like you, who'd like you even more if you'd give them a chance. And you have me."

Luke had been thinking there was something else he hadn't told Cindy. There was one more person who hadn't stood by him, one more who had found it expedient to distance herself from him. A person who had been very special to him at the time. Valerie. Her desertion had hurt, but he'd cut her out of his mind and heart so thoroughly that he hadn't given her more than the most fleeting of thoughts in weeks. Yet he also knew that leftovers of the hurt and anger from that past betrayal lingered. Those bitter residues shouldn't affect his relationship with Cindy. It wasn't fair to burden his growing feelings for her with doubts and reservations from the past. Yet—

Cindy's unexpected and very vigorous physical reaction rattled those thoughts right out of his head. It was hardly possible to think when he was being shaken like a dusty rug. He ducked his head and grabbed her hand, but she kept right on tugging at his ear.

"Damn it, Cindy, what the hell—"

"You are the most stubborn, pessimistic, gloomy—"

She was heading for his other ear, but he managed to ward her off. He got his hands around her wrists, intending to force her hands around behind her. But she twisted in his arms, as slippery and pliable as a strand of spaghetti, and started to scramble away. He grabbed an ankle and worked his way up the leg until he could hold her down with his body half sprawled over hers, a knee anchored between her legs. They were both on their stomachs, the blanket tangled around them.

He wiped sand out of the corner of his mouth. "Okay, I get the picture," he grumbled. "You belong to the silver-lining-in-every-cloud school of thought, and you're mad because I'm not exactly a charter member."

She turned her head to look back over her shoulder at him. Her cheek brushed his chin. "If you ever write a book you can call it *The Power of Negative Thinking,*" she snapped.

"I'm that bad?"

"Worse." Then her voice softened. "Look, you've been wronged. That's obvious. And I'm not naive enough to think there's a nice little silver lining hiding in every unpleasant situation. Sometimes it just isn't there. I'm sympathetic—"

"If this is sympathy, I'd hate to encounter your hard-hearted side."

"This is it. Take it or leave it."

She tried to squirm away again, but he used his greater weight and strength to hold her a moment longer. "Wait. I want to know just one thing."

"What's that?"

"Did you mean what you said?"

"About what?"

He touched the lobe of her ear. So soft. So delicate. An ear made for hearing sweet love words. She had said she loved him. But he couldn't hold her to that powerful a declaration. Not yet. Not until he had his own life more straightened out. But she had also made a less specific statement.

"Did you mean it when you said that I had you?" He planted a hand on either side of her shoulders and lifted his body, giving her the freedom to escape.

The one eye he could see looked wary, as if she wasn't certain she wanted to claim the statement. But finally she did, and she didn't try to escape. "Yes, I meant it."

He lowered his body to hers and kissed that tempting ear, tracing the delicately curved ridges with his tongue. Even after a day on the beach a faint scent of perfume, as sweet and spicy as her name, clung to the hollow behind her earlobe. His tongue probed that hollow, and a quicksilver tremble rippled through her body. He kissed her cheek and temple, the curve of her eyebrow and the corner of her closed eye. She lifted one hand and stroked his cheek as his lips moved down the side of her throat.

"I'm sorry I sounded so gloomy," he whispered.

"I'm glad you finally told me everything. And I'm sorry if I hurt your ear. Did I?"

"Nothing a kiss wouldn't heal."

He shifted his weight, and she turned to face him. She rested her arms on his shoulders, hands meeting behind his neck. Her eyes were open now, their usual blue sparkle transformed into bottomless pools of darkness. She touched his ears again, but this time it was a bare brush of fingertips. She traced the soft outer curve, then caught the lobes and massaged them lightly.

"Better?" she whispered.

"Much better."

Gently she turned his head and lifted her lips to his ear. *Oh, Lord,* Luke thought as the touch shot electricity down his spine. A hot tide instantly surged upward through his muscles to meet it. *Oh, Lord.* Her tongue crept into the sensitive whorl, caressing and exploring and driving him wild. Her lips outlined the outer curve with overlapping kisses, delicately maddening.

The camp fire was almost gone now. Only the dull, red glow of a few embers remained. But the flames weren't gone. They were inside him, licking around his groin, flickering inside his mind. He crushed his pelvis against her, but the sweet torment didn't stop. She nibbled the earlobe with her teeth, the nips just hard enough to make him writhe and squirm in delicious torment. She wrapped her legs around his.

"Cindy... stop...."

"Why?" Her warm breath flooded his ear. It infiltrated his brain like some intoxicating wine. A throb from below echoed each pound of his heartbeat.

He turned his head to look into her eyes. "Because if you don't I'm going to make love to you right here."

She had hesitated before coming to the blanket with him. He'd known from her expression that she was wary of what might happen. But all inhibition was gone from her eyes now, nothing held back. She drew a fingertip across his lips.

"No clocks," she whispered. "No time limits. Just you and me and the beach and the night...."

His mouth claimed hers. She met him halfway, and then her head dropped back to the sand, her hands and mouth drawing him down with her. Her body was soft and giving beneath his, yet he had no feeling of crushing something weak and helpless. Within her feminity was a taut vitality and a muscular agility, and she met him willingly, eagerly.

Her hands worked at the top button of his shirt as they kissed. Luke kicked at the entangling blanket, suddenly wild with impatience to be rid of any barrier between them. He wanted to feel her breasts against his chest, the taut springiness of her belly against his—

The water surged over them in a cold deluge. Luke coughed and sputtered, his mouth full of it.

"What the—" The water swirled and eddied around them. "Cindy, are you all right?"

All light was gone, and the camp fire expired in a final hiss as the water retreated, leaving only a smell of wet, burned wood. He wiped water out of his eyes and still couldn't see anything.

"I'm okay," she said.

"What happened?" he asked. He tried to stand up and found himself tangled in the wet blanket and assorted arms and legs, also wet.

"The tide is coming in. Sometimes an extra-high wave sneaks in ahead of the others."

"Now you tell me."

They unwound themselves from each other and the soggy blanket.

Cold water trickled inside Luke's clothes, chilling the intimate parts of his body that only moments before had felt ready to burst into flame. "We," he muttered unhappily, "have just had the ultimate in cold showers."

Cindy agreed. Never had she felt any less passionate than she did at that moment. Her clothes, hair and skin were soaked. She had a taste of salt water in her mouth and bits of debris and sand in her hair. The wind bit through the wet clothing plastered to her body, instantly chilling her to the bone. And as if the two of them weren't already wet enough, the predicted storm suddenly broke. Another deluge of water hit them from above.

"We'd better get out of here before another wave hits us." Cindy felt around for the Styrofoam ice chest that she'd brought the food in, but she couldn't find it. It was probably sloshing in the surf somewhere. "And before we catch pneumonia or something worse. I'm freezing."

"C'mon now, where's that girl who's always so cheerful about calamity? That girl who thinks rain just makes rainbows, the one who says if life hands you ice, make ice cream."

"Go to hell."

"The girl who says if life gives you mud, make mud pies—"

"If you say one word about clouds and silver linings, I'm going to clobber you with the first thing I can get my hands on." She didn't get her hands on anything, however. She just bumped her bad knee on a chunk of driftwood. She clamped both hands on the joint and moaned as pinpricks of pain stung through the leg, and tears joined rain and sea water on her face. "Oh, damn. Damn."

"Okay, I'll just have to show you the bright side of this little situation, then. Say something so I can find you."

"I can't say anything. I'm so cold my lips won't move."

His outstretched hands found her shoulder and then her hand. Another incoming wave washed around their ankles, and he held on tight. Cindy just followed his lead back to the pickup, not trying to see where she was going. She fished the keys out of the pocket of her jeans and handed them to him.

Luke drove. Cindy just leaned her head back on the seat and wallowed in her cold, wet misery. The fresh scent of sea that she loved on the beach was considerably less appealing when wrapped around two soggy people in the confines of a small pickup cab. They smelled vaguely like leftovers from a fish market.

Luke seemed not to notice smell, chill or wet. He sang a lusty version of "Row, Row, Row Your Boat," occasionally pausing to urge her to join in.

Cindy kept her eyes shut and pretended not to hear.

She didn't open her eyes until the pickup stopped. They weren't in her familiar driveway. She started to protest, but he shushed her and picked her up in his arms.

"We'll pretend this is all just a game," he said as he carried her up the stairs. "I'm a lonely, shipwrecked sailor, and you're the mermaid I found stranded on the beach."

"I don't feel like games," she said grumpily.

Luke carried her directly to the shower. He turned on the water, tested and adjusted it with one hand. Then he placed her fully clothed under the hot spray and stepped in beside her.

The hot water streamed over them. It couldn't get them any wetter than they already were. It sloshed through Cindy's hair and into her clothes. It filled her bra and her pockets, and she tilted her head back and let the spray hit her full in the face. She turned so that it could pummel her backside. Slowly she began to feel less like a lump of waterlogged jetsam washed in on the tide and more like a warm, clean human being. Bits of sea debris, too large to go down the drain, gathered around their feet.

She stepped out of the direct spray and slicked her hair back from her face. Luke had removed his shirt and was now washing it under the shower spray as casually as if that was the way he always did his laundry. His hair hung in a dripping curtain across his forehead, and his wet jeans hugged his pelvis and legs. He flipped the shirt over the shower rod and eyed her with appreciative interest.

"Just what I always wanted," he commented. "My own private wet T-shirt contest."

"You're a little short on entries," she observed.

"I prefer quality to quantity."

"There's something to be said for wet denim, too," she retorted with spirit and a meaningful flick of her eyes. The heavy fabric hadn't the transparency of a wet T-shirt, but it left little to the imagination about his lean build and solid masculinity.

He laughed, unperturbed. "There's also something to be said for taking a shower the normal way," he suggested.

She considered that and inquired, "Alone?"

"Naked," he replied succinctly.

"As I recall, doing it this way was your idea," she pointed out. "I thought that doing bathing and laundry at the same time was perhaps some odd custom you Easterners have."

"Now I have a better idea. Raise your arms."

He deftly skimmed the T-shirt over her head. The almost transparent bra came next, but the tight, wet jeans clung tenaciously to her hips. She let him struggle with them for a while, enjoying the contest, then wriggled out of them. She helped him out of his jeans. She thought he'd take her directly to bed, but he didn't.

Instead he poured creamy shampoo on her hair and worked it into a billowing halo of foam. She just stood there, eyes closed, letting his fingers work unexpected magic on her scalp, feeling the trickle of suds and water and the occasional brush of his body against hers. Why had no one ever told her that heaven was taking a hot shower with the man you loved?

"This is a lovely silver lining," she murmured dreamily. "Worth every second of sloshing in cold surf."

"Sweet Cinnamon, this is only the beginning," he whispered significantly. He was standing behind her, and as he finished his task, his hands slipped over her shoulders and down to her waist. He caught her hips, fingertips pressing into the soft flesh within the curve of her hipbones. He drew her back against him, and there was no mistaking his arousal. "No time limits tonight."

"No time limits," she agreed softly.

She shampooed his hair, and then they toweled each other dry with loving care. She sat on a padded stool in the bedroom, and he blow-dried her hair, lifting the damp, golden strands between his fingers, then letting them fall into a tumble of frothy silk around her shoulders. The warm air seemed almost an extension of him as it caressed her hair and neck and played softly around her ears. She felt warm and rosy and glowed all over. She thought she could sit there forever, lost in the magic caresses of his fingertips and that flowing stream of hot air.

"I'm probably ruining your hairdo," he said as he moved around in front of her to take a critical look. She sat in a spill of light from the bathroom, the remainder of the bedroom in darkness.

His belly was only inches from her face, tantalizing in its nearness. She succumbed to temptation and tugged lightly at the towel. "Who cares about a hairdo?" she murmured. She ran her tongue around the hollow of his navel and drew a fluttery line downward.

And that ended the blow-drying....

He drew her into his arms and kissed her. She wrapped her arms around his neck, feeling a fierce joy in the unrestrained meld of their bodies. He kicked the wooden stool aside and walked her the two steps backward to the bed, then lifted and set her gently on the blue bedspread.

He lay down beside her, his head on the single pillow with hers. He drew her leg over his hip, his hand gently stroking the back of her thigh.

"Do you want the lights out?" he whispered.

"No. I want to look at you."

"But your eyes are closed."

She opened one eye. His nose was almost touching hers. She kissed it, then opened both eyes wide and blinked at him. "There. Satisfied?"

He laughed softly. "That, my love, is a very leading question."

He rose on one elbow and looked down at her as he ran his fingertips lightly across her jaw and throat and around her left breast, and the untouched nipple prickled in eager response. He murmured wordless delight at the inviting response and touched his tongue to the rigid tip. Then he buried his face between her breasts and pulled her on top of himself, arms holding her as if he'd never let her go. She kissed the springy curl of his hair and wrapped her legs around him, the after-bath dampness of their bodies slicking with the heat of desire. She could feel the raw hunger in his kisses and the surge of his body, knew that the wild response of her own body urged him on. But he took an extra moment before fulfilling the pent-up demands of their passion.

"Pill?" he whispered with tactful brevity.

"No."

"I'll take care of it."

He gently set her aside but was back in a moment. She wanted to keep her eyes open, to look deeply into his at the moment when they claimed each other in the act of love. She held him motionless with the pressure of her legs, savoring the moment of ultimate physical contact.

"All night," he whispered. "All night just to make love to you. Your eyes look so huge and dark—" He kissed the curve of her eyebrow.

"Just like yours." And then her eyes drifted shut, and he kissed the closed lids.

He moved gently, and together they savored the newness of each other, aware that what they shared was age-old and yet unique because now it was happening between the two of them. Cindy's passion for this moment had been fiery and demanding, but now she felt the true awakening of the long slumbering depths of her femininity. She felt as if she was blossoming, each movement, each touch and kiss opening a fresh petal of deepening response that was both physical and emotional. She drifted with the sounds of love, the wordless murmurs, the whispers of skin touching skin, the soft kisses.

"Cindy?"

"Mmm?" Her response to his whisper was more contented purr than question.

"Why did we wait so long?"

"Because you had some silly notion about time and deadlines."

"I still want to make love to you all night, but—"

"But?"

The answer was lost in the wild surge of energy and passion that had been building in him and suddenly swept through both of them. Cindy's drifting, dreamy feeling vanished; more specific physical messages emanated from within. She reveled in the hard drive of his body and the strength of her own response. At the last moment he slipped one hand beneath her hips, but it was her own taut muscles that lifted her body to meet his. She cascaded over some precipitous pinnacle within herself and felt him follow to his own peak only moments later.

She drifted in contentment, pleasantly damp, too warm to snuggle but maintaining contact with a link of hands and one leg thrown over his knee.

"You're smiling," Luke whispered.

"I have a right to smile. Aren't you smiling?" She opened one eye. It was too much effort to open both. Yes, he was smiling. Affectionately and possessively. She leaned over and planted a kiss on his damp chest.

"Happy?" he asked.

"Oh, yes!"

"It's been a long time, hasn't it?" He turned on his side to face her. He spread his hand across her abdomen, fingers fanned between her hipbones as if he was absentmindedly measuring the distance.

"A long time since what?" She knew what he meant, but she asked the question, anyway, not certain what to make of his statement.

"Since you made love."

She sat up. "Are you implying that I've forgotten how it's done?" she asked tartly.

He laughed. "No, sweet Cinnamon. You were marvelous. We were marvelous together."

She dropped back, falling within the enclosing circle of his arm. "Yes, we were," she agreed with complacent satisfaction.

"I wasn't implying anything other than that my male intuition tells me it's been a long time. And I suppose, even if it sounds selfish, that I have to admit I'm glad. I could become very jealous of your other lovers, I think." A hint of possessiveness lurked in the words, and his hand slid up to cup her breast with even greater possessiveness. "I'm glad there aren't any current ones."

She hesitated a moment and then said, "There was only one. And you're right, it was a long time ago. I've...avoided physical entanglements since then."

"Were you in love with him?"

"Yes, I think I was. But perhaps I didn't love him enough... or maybe he didn't love me enough. I'm not certain now. Maybe it was just one of those things that wasn't meant to be."

Cindy wasn't particularly eager to delve into the past, but Luke persisted.

"Why not?"

"His name was Jeff, and he moved to Sundust when we were both in junior high. I wasn't going to school there, however. I went to a boarding school over in Texas."

"Why?"

Cindy hesitated again, but there was no way to tell him about what had happened between herself and Jeff without also telling him about her involvement with gymnastics. "So I could take intensive training in gymnastics along with my regular classes. I got home only occasionally on a long weekend or holiday, plus a few weeks during the summer."

"That must have made it rather difficult to keep a teenage romance going."

"Actually, for quite a while it was rather exciting," she reflected. She laughed wryly. "I suppose I was something of a minor celebrity in Sundust. I won a lot of state and regional awards in gymnastics, and everyone made a big fuss when I came home on visits. I was queen of the town's Copperdust Days celebration, and they were always writing about me in the local newspaper. Once the town even raised money to send me to an international gymnastics meet in France. I'd rush in and out of town, and Jeff and I never seemed to get enough of each other."

"And then one time you did see enough of each other, and it was all over?"

"No. After high school, we went to different colleges. Mine was chosen with an eye to how it would help me go on in gymnastics, of course. We continued to see each other when we could manage it, but eventually he found a girl who wasn't all wrapped up in her work the way I was. For me, it came down to a choice between gymnastics and Jeff . . . I chose gymnastics." As an afterthought she added, "I understand he's married now and has a little boy." She was glad for him. He was a good guy and deserved a good wife and happiness.

"You're a very good gymnast, of course."

Cindy stiffened warily. "What makes you say that?"

"Because I saw you."

A sudden silence, broken only by a rhythmic drip-drip from the leaky shower head in the bathroom.

He must have seen her at the beach some night. She couldn't remember exactly when she'd last gone there to practice, but it had been at least several weeks ago. She didn't go often, because she had to be careful not to strain her bad knee. "Why didn't you ever mention it?"

"It was before we met. I was down at the beach one night, and I saw you...only I didn't know it was you then, of course...in the moonlight. I was fascinated. Thrilled. I wanted to meet the woman who could perform such beautiful, graceful moves. But it didn't take any great insight to see that the woman was there alone and at night because she didn't want an audience."

Cindy was shocked. Of course a few people knew she'd been involved with gymnastics at one time, but she'd been careful to keep those occasional sessions on the beach very private. Gymnastics was a part of the painful past that she'd abandoned...although she hadn't been able to abandon that past completely. Sometimes she was drawn to the exhilaration of the old routines and flying moves as if they were some vitamin or stimulant that she couldn't live without.

She momentarily resented the fact that Luke had accidentally spied on her, but at the same time felt a deep respect and admiration for his sensitivity. Not many men would have sensed what he had and been thoughtful enough not to intrude on her privacy.

"Then, after I met you, I saw similarities between you and the woman on the beach, but there were differences, too. She was all moonlight and magic and mystery—"

"And what am I?" she challenged, absurdly miffed, even though this other woman he was talking about was also herself. "Fun and games in a wet T-shirt?"

"Yes, you're that," he agreed, smiling fondly. He circled her breast with a fingertip. "And much, much more. I was always a little afraid to ask if you were that woman on the beach because I thought you might turn and run, the way she seemed ready to do that night."

Cindy didn't comment on whether or not she might have done just that at some earlier point in their relationship.

"Will you do a private performance for me sometime?" he asked. "One where I don't have to hide behind a rock to watch you?"

She didn't commit herself. "I'll think about it."

"Why do you do this all alone, where no one can see you?"

"Oh, I'm not as good as I once was. . . ." she answered, purposely vague.

"I've seen a few scars around your knee. Did you hurt it in a fall or something?"

The night he'd seen her, the knee had apparently given her no problems, but that wasn't always the case. Sometimes there was a fall, one that left her with tears of both pain and frustration. She didn't care to share that frustration any more than she cared to share the story of her failure.

"What goes up must come down. That's especially true in gymnastics," she said lightly.

"Why did you stop competing?"

"And why don't you, Luke Townsend, stop talking so much?" she chastised him with mock severity. She leaned over him, deliberately distracting him with a tantalizing brush of breasts against his chest. She kissed him on the corner of the mouth, the tip of her tongue flirting with the parted line of his lips. "You promised me a night of love, and now all you want to do is talk, talk, talk. . . ."

7

LUKE WAS UP FIRST the next morning. He started bacon cooking and coffee perking. A few minutes later, when the aromas drifted into the bedroom, he heard Cindy stirring. She came out of the bedroom wearing an old blue shirt of his, sleeves rolled up, shirttails pulled snug around her bottom and knotted in front. She looked sleepy, deliciously disheveled and more appetizing than breakfast. Her bare feet and shapeless shirt only emphasized the length of her slim legs. She ran a hand through her hair, yawned and smiled lazily.

"I do believe I could become addicted to waking up and finding a handsome man cooking breakfast," she said. She lifted her head and sniffed appreciatively.

He set the fork on the counter and draped his arms around her. He was wearing clean dry jeans, no shirt. His wet clothes from the night before were still puddled with hers on the bathroom floor. Her breasts felt soft and warm, delightfully mobile with only the barrier of the shirt between them and his bare skin. "I'm already addicted. And it has nothing to do with food." He lowered his hands to the curve of her bottom and lifted her lightly against him. His good intentions about lovingly bringing her breakfast in bed floundered under the assault of a more potent desire.

"To hell with breakfast," he muttered with rough tenderness. "Let's go back to bed."

"I can't. I have to work this morning, and you know how you are about deadlines and time limits and things like that." The teasing in her eyes belied the primness of her voice. She walked her bare feet on top of his and rested her forearms on his collarbone. She fixed her gaze on his eyes as if to say this phobia of his was a truly perplexing problem.

"It's pouring down rain out there. No one is even thinking about buying a kite today."

"The store still has to be open." She ran a fingertip across his lower lip, and Luke knew that in spite of the tantalizing breakfast aromas and the talk of work, she had other things on her mind, too. "But I suppose I *might* be persuaded to call Joanna and ask her to open up this morning," she added with assumed carelessness.

With one hand Luke turned off the heat under the bacon. With the other he unfastened the top button of the old shirt. He kissed the hollow of her throat. He unfastened the other buttons and slid his hands inside the shirt. He squeezed her breasts lightly together and kissed the soft line where they met.

"Yes," she murmured in a conversational tone, "I think I will definitely call Joanna. . . ."

He carried her to the bedroom and snuggled his body around hers while she dialed from the phone on the nightstand.

"Joanna? Hi. Something has come up, and I'm running a little late this morning. Would it be possible for you to open the shop?"

Cindy sounded briskly businesslike, so controlled, giving no hint that what had come up was their mutual passion, and that Luke was nibbling the side of her throat. He untied the shirttails and slipped the oversize sleeve from her arm. He kissed the smooth curve of her back and ran his tongue down the rippled line of her spine.

She said something to Joanna about the mail and then added, "You probably won't be busy on a day like this, so you can..." He nudged his head under her arm and kissed the side of her breast, and her voice drifted off. There was only the sound of her soft breathing as his tongue crept toward her nipple.

Then, in response to something Joanna said, Cindy jerked upright. "What? Yes, of course I'm fine." She gave Luke a reprimanding jab with her elbow. "Something just distracted me for a moment. You can unpack those new mylar kites if you have time."

Joanna apparently asked something about the invoice, and Cindy answered. She threw a dark look over her shoulder, but Luke just grinned and kept on kissing her. He nibbled on her hip and the nape of her neck and various points in between, until finally, sounding a little frantic, she ended the conversation.

"I think, uh, that something is about to…burn. I'll see you a little later, okay?"

She slammed down the phone and turned to Luke. "How do you expect me to carry on a business conversation when you're making love to me?" she demanded a little indignantly.

"How do you expect me to make love to you when you're carrying on a business conversation?" he returned. "Besides, that wasn't making love to you. *This* is making love to you."

He lowered his body over hers, watching as her blue eyes grew soft and blurry and then drifted shut. And then his own closed, and he kissed her, and the only sounds were those of love.

AFTERWARD THEY FINISHED cooking and eating the delayed breakfast. While Cindy showered, Luke drove over to the cottage and picked up fresh clothes for her. He finally delivered her to the kite shop at about eleven o'clock. No cars were parked outside, and the big green wind sock with the store's name hung wet and limp in the rain.

He reached across and opened the door.

"Luke, I suppose I should confess something. . . ."

Luke felt dismay twist a hard knot in his stomach. He'd pretty well convinced himself that Cindy was different from those "friends" he'd known, but sometimes he sensed a layer to her character that he'd never penetrated. What had she to confess?

"Oh?" he responded warily.

"That morning when we came back from Portland and you undressed me? I wasn't really asleep."

He relaxed. Sweet Cinnamon. So honest and uncomplicated. "I know." His tone was fondly amused.

"You *knew*?" Then, after a moment's frowning concentration, "I suppose I should have guessed. Even an amateur doesn't need to do that much fumbling and feeling around to remove a dress. So why did you let me think—"

"And deprive myself of all the fun of undressing you? But if it will make you feel better, sometime I'll pretend to be asleep, and *you* can—"

She wrinkled her nose at him and dashed to the door of the shop. She turned and blew him a kiss before ducking inside.

The day was cold, rainy and depressing, but Luke didn't feel in the least depressed. He felt good, buoyant . . . and not just because making love had momentarily satiated him. For almost the first time since he'd left his job with the Marianna Funds, he felt real optimism about the future. Hell, he'd thought so long and bitterly about all he'd lost that he hadn't bothered to take inventory of what remained. Maybe, as Cindy said, he'd been too pessimistic.

He still had his education and the skills he'd learned at Marianna. He'd kept up on what was going on in the stock market, even though he'd dropped out of that world. Cindy was right in saying he had a good job at the mill. It was decent, honest work, nothing to be ashamed of. But he didn't want to pull green chain all his life. Maybe a fresh start really was possible.

THE RAIN SETTLED over the coast as if the clouds were permanently snagged on the coastal mountains. It came down all week, sometimes a deluge, sometimes a drizzle, but always there. Even the weekend was slow at the kite shop. Cindy gave the other clerks time off and used her own extra time to create a fresh window display and sort out some slow-selling kites to put on sale. She also sent a new kite design up to the main store in Astoria for consideration, wishing she'd thought of it earlier so that it could have been developed in time for the sand-sculpture festival. It was by far her most ambitious design, but she had no idea what her boss might think of a kite shaped like a sand castle!

Pam and Kylie came in one afternoon to buy a kite as a birthday present for Pam's niece in Massachusetts. Kylie commented that they ought to get their group together and decide what sort of sand sculpture they were going to do for that year's festival. Cindy agreed and said she'd get in touch with some of the others.

In an aside, Pam said, "My, you look all glowy these days."

Joanna had said nearly the same thing, grumbling that it was almost indecent to look so cheerful in this dismal weather. Cindy had just murmured something noncommittal to Joanna, but she knew it would take more than raindrops to douse the sunshine of new love that shone inside her.

She saw Luke every day, although sometimes it was only for a few minutes. He was in an upbeat mood that matched her own, and he was as ready as she was to snatch their lovemaking in whatever minutes they could arrange—no more talk of waiting until there were no deadlines! He was also a little secretive, but it was a different kind of secrecy this time, as if he was holding back something nice to surprise her with later. Now she just said airily in response to Pam's reference, "It must be the new vitamins I just started taking."

Pam's small, conspiratorial grin said she knew exactly what "vitamin" that was.

Finally, one evening when Cindy and Luke were finishing dinner at an elegant inn down the coast from Steller Beach, he revealed the secret he'd been holding back. The evening had felt like a celebration, even though she hadn't known what there was to celebrate. They'd eaten the specialties of the house, wild rice seasoned with herbs and Indian baked salmon with a brown sugar glaze. Candlelight flickered in his dark eyes as he set down his wineglass and made his announcement.

"I have an appointment next week to discuss a job with a stock brokerage firm in Portland."

Cindy felt only the smallest of twinges at the thought of his moving to Portland. With honest delight she said, "Luke, that's terrific! Congratulations. How did it happen?"

"Maybe I was shamed into it by my beautiful bed partner." As if it were a matter of the utmost importance, he added thoughtfully, "Whatever made us think we wanted to invest in a pair of those skinny little twin beds?"

"From what I've seen, we have space left over in those skinny little beds," Cindy answered tartly. "But stop changing the subject and tell me what this is all about."

"After your rather unladylike ear pulling a while back, I worked up a résumé, had it typed by a secretarial service downtown and submitted copies to several brokerage firms in Portland. They were pretty much shots in the dark, of course, because I didn't know of any actual job openings, but one firm responded. They said they were impressed with my résumé and wanted to meet me."

"I'm so happy for you. That really is marvelous."

"Aren't you even a *trifle* upset at the thought that the firm is located in Portland?"

Cindy looked down and twisted her wineglass in half-moon curves on the heavy white tablecloth. Of course it bothered her, but she was glad to see that he was putting his anger and bitterness behind him. Carefully she asked, "Does it upset you?"

"No." But he didn't give her time to get angry over the complacent reply. "Because if I get the job I'll be working here on the coast. They're planning to open a branch office, probably not in Steller Beach—it's too small—but not far away."

"The news gets better all the time!"

He sobered suddenly and stared at his empty wineglass. "Yeah. Well, that was the good news. Now the bad news."

Cindy just tilted her head and waited. She suspected what it was.

"I didn't tell them why I left Marianna or what happened there. I just ignored it on the résumé. But in the interview I'll have to tell them, of course. They'll check my references and find out, anyway, and I don't want it to look as if I'm hiding anything."

"It's possible the people at Marianna will never mention it," Cindy suggested thoughtfully. "After all, you were found innocent."

"Are you saying *I* shouldn't mention it?"

Cindy shook her head and sighed. "No. You're right. Even if the embezzlement charge didn't happen to come up before you were hired, you'd always be worrying that they might find out later. It just seems so unfair. It's a negative thing you don't deserve."

"Life is tough," Luke observed philosophically but not resentfully. He smiled tolerantly. "But you wouldn't know about that, would you? You just sail through life flying your kites and intriguing strangers on the beach in the moonlight."

Cindy smiled faintly. "Yes, that's me. Charter member of the smile-and-the-world-smiles-with-you club." Abruptly she changed the subject. "Since you're in such a good humor, I have a question to ask you."

"Something obscene, I hope?" He exaggerated a hopeful leer.

"Not unless you find digging in the sand obscene. I just wondered if you'd like to be on our team to enter the sand-sculpture contest. We're planning to get together in a few days to decide what we want to build this year. We're short several team members."

It was a good time to hit Luke with the proposal. He grinned. "Sure. Why not? Sounds like fun. They give prizes?"

"We probably won't win anything," Cindy warned. "We do it just because it *is* fun. And we like to support the town's activities, of course. The festival draws lots of tourists."

"Who buy kites."

"Now you're making me sound mercenary."

"Who says you can't have fun and be a bit mercenary, too?"

JOANNA, BECAUSE OF HER PREGNANCY, had decided not to take part this year, but her husband, Max, was still on the team, and they invited everyone to their house for the organizational meeting. Joanna's sister-in-law, Melanie, had asked if she could take Joanna's place. Melanie's husband couldn't participate, however. He'd found a job driving a truck, a temporary job but seven days a week while it lasted.

Melanie brought the kids to the meeting, where they clustered around Luke as if he were some long-lost uncle and clamored to know when they were going to build another fort. Then little Tracy turned to Cindy.

"I tried 'n tried to do an errol cartwheel," she announced. "But I can't do it."

Cindy looked at her blankly. "An errol cartwheel?"

"I think she means aerial," Luke interjected. "The last time we were at the beach, you asked her if she could do an aerial cartwheel."

"Can you show me how?" the little girl prodded.

Cindy hesitated and then answered more curtly than Luke would have expected. "Maybe sometime. We'll see."

Pam and Kylie arrived, and the meeting more or less came to order when the final participants, Susan and Jet Schraft, arrived on a motorcycle. Jet's nickname, although not his pleasantly pudgy appearance, fitted the powerful roar of his machine. Luke had seen him around the mill, and they nodded cordially to each other. Everyone sprawled around the big living room, and the kids were shooed into the kitchen for soft drinks and cookies while the adults discussed the project.

There was a total of eight team members. That was two less than they'd had the year before, Max pointed out.

"Will that be a problem?" Luke asked.

"Last year we were falling all over each other because there were so many of us," Pam said. She eyed Luke as if she might like to fall all over him, and Cindy gave her a dark look.

Luke just smiled at Pam's sultry glance. He had already figured out that she was all talk and no action, not that it mattered one way or the other to him. He looked to Cindy for comment.

"I think there are plenty of us. The big question now is, what are we going to build for this year's contest?" Cindy said.

Pam and Kyle had brought along snapshots, taken at last year's festival. They passed them around. Luke was surprised at how large, complicated and inventive the sand sculptures were. There were numerous sand castles, of course, complete with turrets, domes, arched gates, winding stairs and miniature forests. There were other structures, too: a sphinx, a White House and an Alamo. In the noncastle category were various whimsical creations: a grinning gorilla, a graceful trio of seals and an old truck with one wheel appropriately stuck in the sand.

And there was the infamous two-headed dragon, minus one head, attacking a castle. The team members were gathered in a semicircle around it, smiling in spite of the small disaster.

The winning sculptures were marked by plaques, and Luke noted that one thing they had in common was a sharply defined, carved look, almost as if they had been chiseled out of the sand. That seemed as important in the judging as intricacy of design.

"We could do the two-headed dragon attacking the castle again, and this year get it *right*," Kylie suggested.

Pam groaned. "I spent hours creating about a million little scales on that dumb dragon's back. No more dragons."

They explored several more ideas. Melanie suggested sculptures of a couple of children flying one of Cindy's kites, but Cindy reminded them that such manufactured props weren't allowed. Jet suggested a replica of a motorcycle, which didn't seem to interest anyone. Max said they needed something big and impressive, without a lot of tiny detail that dried and crumbled too quickly.

"How about something along the same line as the dragon attacking the castle, but just a little different...maybe a giant octopus coming up out of the sea to attack a lighthouse?" Luke suggested.

That got a quick positive response all around. Luke was pleased until everyone started asking questions, and he realized that his casual suggestion apparently meant that he was supposed to supervise the whole project.

"Hey, wait a minute!" he objected, good-naturedly but vehemently. "Back off. I don't know a thing about how to build something out of sand."

"It isn't technical advice we need. It's management," Cindy pointed out. "Someone to coordinate our efforts. Look what a great supervisor you were on the kids' fort-building project the other day."

"Right," Melanie chimed in. "Anyone who can organize that gang into doing anything gets my vote."

They made a list of tools they'd need, a list that amazed Luke, and of who was to supply what; shovels, buckets, trowels, spoons, spatulas, water sprayers.

"And food," Jet put in, revealing where his true interest lay. "We gotta have refreshments to keep up our energy."

Cindy said she'd research pictures of lighthouses and pick a suitable design. They then decided a practice session was necessary and chose an evening the following week, the same day as Luke's morning appointment with the stock brokerage firm in Portland. The weather was supposed to clear up by then. They had a lengthy if none too serious discussion about where to hold this session so as to avoid the spying eyes of unprincipled competitors, and finally chose a secluded beach north of town for the rendezvous.

On the drive home, Luke shook his head and laughed. "Somehow I never envisioned myself holding the position of supervisor on a project to construct a lighthouse and octopus out of sand."

"You'll be terrific," Cindy assured him. "We'll be terrific together, just as we are at...mmm...other endeavors." She leaned over and kissed him on the cheek.

And then they went back to the cottage and proved again just how terrific they were.

CINDY DIDN'T SAY ANYTHING to Luke, but she worried about his interview. Not that she hadn't every confidence in his ability to do the job if he got it, but handling people's money was such a sensitive area that it might not be easy to overcome that past accusation, unfair as it had been. She was privately less optimistic than she let on to Luke.

Yet when he picked her up at the kite store at closing time, the day of the interview and the sand-building session, she didn't have to ask to know that everything had gone satisfactorily. It showed in his easy smile and relaxed expression. But she did ask, because she wanted to hear the reassuring words.

"Everything went all right? You got the job?"

"Everything went beautifully. But I won't know for a couple of weeks or so about the job." He sounded confident.

"You told them about what happened at Marianna?"

"Yes."

"What did they say?"

"Well, not much. But they didn't throw up their hands in horror or turn me down on the spot. The man who interviewed me was noncommittal, but he seemed understanding."

"Great! I brought you a little present." She handed him a sack.

He opened it and pulled out a blue cap. Across the front in blazing silvery letters was the word King.

"King?" he questioned. *"King?"*

"Well, the title of supervisor seemed so ordinary for your exalted position as manager of our project. I thought we needed a touch of class, so I made you king."

"The sand castle king. Too bad I didn't know earlier so I could add the title to my résumé. I'm sure that would have impressed them."

"You've always impressed me . . . even before you were a king."

He grinned and stuck the cap on his head at a jaunty angle. They went by the cottage so that Cindy could change clothes, then headed for the secluded beach.

The cap was an immediate hit. Cindy suspected that Luke felt a little foolish with everyone calling him King, but he took it good-naturedly.

The late-spring evenings were long now, but still cool, and the first thing they did was start a warming fire blazing. Cindy noted that Luke was careful to place it above the high-tide line. The kids and their inevitable companion, the dog, raced up and down the beach.

Cindy had a photo of an old lighthouse to use as a guide for the project. It was an angular, four-sided structure with a large base sloping up to a narrower peak. A catwalk surrounded the structure just below the windows.

"First, how much time will we have to build this thing?" Luke asked briskly.

"I'm already impressed," Pam said. "Remember two years ago when we did that gorgeous Edinburgh Castle—except we were only half done when the judging started?"

Cindy explained that the contestants could start building at seven a.m. The judging started about one o'clock, with the winners announced at two. "That's more time than we'll have this evening, so if we can get it done tonight we know we'll have plenty of time that day."

"Now let's work out some measurements," Luke said. "How tall is this thing going to be?"

They decided the lighthouse should be seven feet high, which meant they were going to have to move a lot of sand. Luke suggested that everyone should help pile up the bulk of sand required, and then the women could work on the finer points of sculpting it into a lighthouse shape while the men started on the octopus.

Everyone pitched in, and the pile of sand grew quickly, although there were numerous AWOL's for refreshments. The sand was wet and heavy and compacted nicely. They didn't need the water sprayers to keep it damp that evening. Cindy worked steadily, but out of the corner of her eye she kept watching Tracy.

Tracy played with the same blithe energy that the other children did, but every once in a while she'd try to do an "errol" cartwheel. Inevitably she'd take a tumble, but soon she'd try it again. Cindy could see what she was doing wrong. Her little rump was stuck out, throwing her off balance, and she wasn't pushing off right. A couple of times Cindy almost went over to show Tracy what she was doing wrong, but each time she stopped. Teaching gymnastics to children had been another of her failures, a job she'd decided to quit before she got fired.

Yet Tracy's persistence finally got to her. The poor little thing was going to have sand burns from all the tumbles she was taking! Mumbling an excuse about getting something to drink, she left the construction project and walked over to where Tracy was roughhousing with the dog.

She pointed out what the girl was doing wrong with her aerial cartwheels. Tracy listened, but instead of accepting the instruction gratefully, she looked skeptical.

"Can *you* do it?"

"I can if I'm properly warmed up . . . and if I want to."

"So why don't you?"

"Maybe I just don't want to. I have important things to do." Cindy frowned and gestured toward the sand sculpture.

"I don't think you can do it." The little girl folded her arms across her chest, looking for all the world like a miniature of a stonehearted gymnastics coach Cindy had once had. "You're just braggin'."

Cindy glared at her, did a couple of standard cartwheels and then flew through the aerial maneuver twice. "See?"

The little girl grinned mischievously, and Cindy knew she'd been had. She'd just been outwitted by one little eight-year-old daredevil.

"Now let's see you do it," Cindy said. "I'll help you."

Tracy failed several more times, but finally with Cindy helping she made it. The movement had no style, but it was strong and bold. Cindy felt an odd rush of pride. She gave the little girl a quick, congratulatory hug. What wouldn't Tracy be able to do with a little real training!

"That's terrific. Maybe you'll go to the Olympics someday."

"Did you go to the 'lympics? I watched some on TV." She jumped on a narrow log and pirouetted as if it was a balance beam. She had remarkable natural balance.

"No, sweetie, I never did go to the Olympics." At one time it would have hurt to admit that, but the statement was merely factual now, without emotional content. She was a little surprised that Tracy was familiar with Olympic competition. She had been at that age, of course, but she had already been working with a professional trainer. "I have to get back to work now. But you keep practicing and remember what I told you, okay?"

Tracy raced off, blond hair flying, a tiny tumbleweed of a girl. Once Cindy would have envied all that agility and energy, but now she just smiled and shook her head fondly at the little girl's antics.

She went back to work on the lighthouse. If her activity with Tracy had been noticed, it wasn't mentioned.

The practice session was fun if, in the final analysis, not overly productive. The catwalk fell off the lighthouse, and the octopus had some thick and some thin arms. It also looked as if it was hugging rather than attacking the lighthouse. Kylie, with Pam astride his shoulders to put the finishing touches on the peak, got to horsing around, and then both fell into the octopus's head. Evening light had faded to darkness by the time the team gave up on the project for the night, and the incoming tide was heading toward their considerably less than artistic creation.

Everyone stood around the fire for a few minutes, discussing plans for the festival, and then the gathering broke up. Jet and Susan stayed longer than the others. There was some food remaining that Jet apparently was determined not to let go to waste. But finally even they roared off, the sound of their motorcycle growing fainter until it faded into the night and only the sea sounds remained.

"I'm afraid your royal subjects don't take their work too seriously," Cindy apologized.

"Oh, well, as everyone keeps saying, it's all just for fun, anyway," Luke said philosophically.

Cindy was glad he'd adopted that attitude. She laughed. "I don't think we need worry about anyone stealing our ideas or techniques, at least. We should probably be spying on some better team."

"I wasn't spying, but I saw you and Tracy. I'll bet you'd make a great gymnastics teacher."

Cindy momentarily reflected on that odd rush of pride that Tracy's accomplishment had given her. It was certainly a different feeling than she'd had when she was working as an assistant at her coach's gymnastics school. Back then she'd been ashamed of the way she felt, often more envious than helpful toward those gymnastic hopefuls, but the unlovely emotion had been there, nonetheless. This feeling of pride was indeed different.

But there was no point in dwelling on that difference. She'd had her chance at teaching and blown it. That was all part of the past.

She distracted both her own and Luke's thoughts by lifting his arm and draping it around her shoulders. "And I'll bet you that if we were to snuggle up by the fire this time, the surf wouldn't give us a cold shower. . . ."

He grinned and swept her up in his arms. "My thoughts exactly."

8

THE TEAM GOT TOGETHER one more time to refine their plans before the sand-sculpture festival. They discussed how to keep the catwalk from collapsing and, with Jet's prodding, what food to take. They also ganged up on Pam and Kylie with dire threats about what would happen if the pair overslept and straggled in late again that year. They pooled resources to come up with the small entry fee, and a couple of days later Cindy officially entered them as The Windy Bunch.

The pace around Steller Beach picked up now that the summer tourist season was beginning to bloom. Business was lively; there was always a nice stream of customers into the shop after one of Cindy's kite-flying demonstrations at the town beach. Luke often tagged along when his working and sleeping hours allowed, but he just laughed and shook his head when she asked if he'd like to learn to fly one of the stunt kites that always fascinated people.

There was a certain barrier of resistance in him, a stubborn line he wouldn't step across, even though his behavior was considerably more easygoing and relaxed these days. He still considered kite flying a little too frivolous, a little too juvenile, Cindy realized regretfully.

She was a little miffed that he sometimes seemed more interested in a new company that had just opened offices in town, a company that would use wind power in a more practical way than she did. Once the firm got through all the red tape of permits and regulations, it was planning to build a number of wind turbines in an isolated canyon down the coast. The same wind power that she employed to fly her kites would be harnessed to provide a clean, commercial source of electrical energy. The company was looking for investors, and Luke said that if he'd had any money he would certainly have put something into the project. He sounded frustrated, and she was reminded again of all he'd lost.

In spite of hoping that he would get the job he was being considered for, she sometimes wondered uneasily if he wouldn't slip back into his old workaholic ways once he started work in the competitive stock market field again. But although he was maintaining a no-news-is-good-news optimism, he had heard nothing from the Portland company.

The number of visitors in Steller Beach began to swell several days before the weekend of the festival. By the day before, every motel room and every campsite and recreational vehicle spot was filled, and sidewalks, restaurants and shops overflowed with people. The usually slow-moving town jumped with activity. Cindy was sorry that Joanna wasn't going to be on the sand sculpture team this year but at the same time relieved that she could leave the kite shop in her capable hands for the day.

Cindy kept the shop open late the evening before the Saturday contest, with gratifying results in sales. Especially popular was an inexpensive kite she'd designed, a diamond shape in a variety of colors with a picture of a sand castle printed on it. She dashed out for a sandwich about six o'clock, then closed up at nine. The lumber mill where Luke worked had shut down for the weekend, a civic gesture made so that the employees could participate in the festival.

Cindy was surprised that Luke hadn't appeared by the time she locked up. She'd been so busy that it wasn't until then that she realized she hadn't seen or heard from him all day. They were planning to go to the street dance, and music already blared from an enthusiastic country-and-western band playing atop a makeshift stage erected at the far end of the street. In spite of a long, hard day on her feet, she was rejuvenated by the music and the mood of good-time exhilaration in the air. She felt like dancing!

Cindy wove her way through the boisterous crowd and headed toward her pickup in the parking lot. She met Pam and Kylie, who were obviously preparing to spend the night dancing rather than resting up for digging in the sand the next day.

"Hey, where's the King?" Kylie called.

"Oh, he's around somewhere. No doubt tending to some king-type business," she called back gaily.

But inside she was a bit annoyed with Luke. The street dance was half the fun of the festival, and they were missing it. She finally got her pickup out of the parking lot and threaded her way through the streets jammed with traffic. As soon as she got home, she dialed his number but there was no answer.

Her annoyance shifted to concern. It seemed very odd that he hadn't called if something had come up.

Going over to his apartment seemed pointless. If he was there he'd surely have answered the phone. Yet on instinct she drove over there, anyway, and somehow she wasn't too surprised to find his car parked at the bottom of the outside stairs. From the minute she'd heard the ringing of his phone in her ear, she'd had the shivery intuition that something was very wrong.

She dashed up the stairs and knocked. Even from here she could hear the faint sound of the dance music. Its cheerful rowdiness contrasted with the ominous silence from the apartment. She knocked again.

A moment later the outdoor light came on, and Luke opened the door. He looked as if he'd put on jeans just to answer the door. The top button wasn't fastened. He was barefoot and shirtless, hair tousled, eyes still heavy with sleep.

"We were supposed to go to the street dance. I tried to call, but you didn't answer."

He looked at his digital watch as if the numbers were unfamiliar. She had a sudden, dismayed feeling that she shouldn't have come. She was in love with him, but he'd never said the words, and they'd never made any commitments. "Are you . . . alone?" she asked, half afraid a sleepy female face might suddenly peer around his bare shoulder.

He pulled the door back and stepped aside. "Of course I'm alone." His voice held a what-the-hell-are-you-talking-about? irritation, and she felt a twinge of guilt. He looked at the watch again. "I'm sorry about the dance. I intended to lie down just for a few minutes. I hadn't had any sleep since I got off work this morning. I didn't hear the phone."

"It's not too late to go to the dance. But we don't have to if you're tired, of course," she added quickly.

He turned away. "I guess I don't feel much like dancing."

"Did something . . . happen?"

He laughed humorlessly. He switched on the kitchen light, swished a half-full pot of cold coffee and then turned on the burner under it. "One guess what."

She leaned against the kitchen counter. "You didn't get the job."

"Right. I wonder what the hell ever made me imagine I would get it."

"What happened?"

He nodded toward a torn envelope on the counter. Cindy opened it and unfolded the sheet inside. The letter was brief, polite and cool. It merely said that the company had decided against hiring him for the new office they were opening on the coast. She turned the letter over, realizing as she did that it was a foolish gesture. Some illuminating explanation wasn't going to be hidden in fine print on the back. And she knew all too well what the explanation was.

Carefully she refolded the letter and tucked it back in the envelope. "So it's a turndown. There must be lots of other stock brokerage companies. There'll be other openings."

"Right. And when they contact Marianna Funds about my past performance record, they'll get exactly the same kind of reference letter about me that this company got."

"How do you know what kind of reference Marianna gave you? The letter doesn't say—"

"I received this letter in the morning mail. My first instinct was to jam it in the trash and forget it. But then I decided I wasn't going to let it go at that."

"What did you do?"

The coffee started to boil. It smelled strong and acrid. He took the pot off the burner. "I obviously wasn't getting the job, so I didn't see much need for tact or diplomacy. I drove to the office in Portland, marched in and asked point-blank if the rejection had anything to do with the reference from my former employer. After some hemming and hawing around, they finally admitted that it did. I demanded to see what Marianna had written about me. After a short conference, they decided to let me see it." He smiled with grim humor.

Probably thinking that Luke might tear the place apart if they didn't, Cindy suspected. Something of that intimidating fury still radiated from him, disquieting in its intensity, even though she knew it wasn't directed at her.

"What did it say?"

He poured two cups of coffee and handed one to her. "About what I expected."

"Luke, if they're disseminating false information about you, you surely have a legal case against them. They can't do that!" The familiar anger and fierce protectiveness surged through her again at this fresh injustice. Hadn't they already done enough to him? She clenched the coffee cup, overcome by an irrational need to fling it at whoever was doing this to him.

"They didn't say anything that wasn't absolutely true. I imagine their lawyers went over the statement. They said my work had been satisfactory. That took all of one line. They took a lot more lines to say that I had been accused of embezzlement, tried and found innocent." He took a long gulp of the coffee, not seeming to notice that it was still too hot to drink. "They also pointed out *how* I had been found innocent, that I chose to leave the company of my own volition—and that no other person had ever been apprehended for the crime."

Every word totally true. Cruelly vindictive—but no doubt legal. Cindy didn't need to be told what this did not only to his hopes for the future but to his slowly improving attitude toward people, as well.

She went over and put her arms around his waist. She had no platitudes to offer, but she did have her love. He put his arms around her, too, but it felt like an automatic, almost absentminded gesture.

"Have you eaten?" she asked.

"I'll fix some eggs and toast or something."

"I'll do it for you."

"And tell me things will look brighter tomorrow?"

Cindy ignored the bitter question. He was angry and hurting again, and he was striking out at her; it didn't mean anything. "Do you want to skip the sand sculpture contest tomorrow?"

"No. I'll be there. What's a team without its king?" The question held no humor, however, only more of the same mocking bite.

"Would you like me to stay here tonight?"

"I don't think I'll be very good company tonight." It wasn't an outright rejection, but it got his point across. He patted her shoulder in a be-a-good-little-girl gesture. "I'll come over to the cottage tomorrow morning. We need your pickup to carry the tools. We'll also need a stepladder to reach the top of the lighthouse. I don't want Pam and Kylie clowning around and messing up everything."

His talk about the next day didn't relieve Cindy. He sounded grim, as if the contest was some hostile obstacle to be surmounted. His next words reinforced that impression.

"And if you run into any of your friends, tell them to be prepared to work. We're going to win something tomorrow."

He put a faint but significant emphasis on *your*. Now they were her friends again, not his. She started to protest. That wasn't fair! He was lumping the guilty and innocent together again. But she held back the words, knowing he wouldn't really hear them at this point. Maybe later, after he'd cooled down. Except that he was already too cool, as remote as an ice sculpture.

He walked down to the pickup with her and leaned through the window to kiss her good-night. For a moment something flared between them, a quick, hot flash of passion, sharp and stinging. His mouth clamped down on hers. It was Cindy who pulled away. She had wanted to spend the night with him when she'd offered, but didn't want to use sex to ensnare him if he didn't really want her around.

"You will eat something?"

"What is it that makes women think food cures everything?" He saw the hurt trembling of her lips in response to the unwarranted crack and apologized. "I'm sorry. Yes, I'll eat something. Why don't you go on back to the street dance? I'll see you tomorrow."

She started the engine. "Sure. See you tomorrow."

She didn't go to the dance, of course. She'd lost all desire to dance. The music, faintly audible in the distance from her cottage driveway, sounded twangy and a bit tawdry now.

For the first time that she could remember, she was not particularly looking forward to the sand castle contest.

LUKE KNOCKED on her door before six the following morning. Cindy was up, but just barely. She was still in her cinnamon-colored shortie nightgown, but the see-through froth had no effect on him. He was strictly business this morning. She might have been wearing a cardboard box for all the notice he took. He was wearing the King cap, but there was no hint of playfulness about him.

"Do you have the pickup loaded?"

"Luke, for heaven's sake, we can't start doing anything before seven o'clock. That's the rule."

"I want to get started on time. We have to sign in or something, don't we? Do you have the shovels and buckets in?"

"Yes, the pickup is loaded. Except for the stepladder. It's in the carport."

"I'll get it."

Cindy dressed and hurried through scrambled eggs and toast. As she'd suspected, no other members of their team had yet arrived when she and Luke reached the beach. Quite a few people were already milling around, but they were one of the first teams to be assigned a plot of sand, a square twenty-two feet on each side. They also received their whimsical Building Permit stickers that showed they were registered contestants. Cindy planted a pole bearing a bright red wind sock with The Windy Bunch painted on it. There was little breeze on this cool, foggy morning, and the wind sock hung there, looking as dispirited as Cindy felt. The tide was heading out. Figures melted in and out of the fog. Cindy had heard there were almost a hundred teams competing in the various categories.

A temporary rope fence had been erected around the outside perimeter of the plots to keep the crowds of onlookers out of the actual building areas. The individual plots within the larger area were marked with corner stakes but not fenced off, so Luke efficiently outlined the boundary of their area with string. He obviously had no intention of letting anyone grab a few spoonfuls of his sand. Cindy thought about teasing him about being so proprietary but didn't. His set face precluded teasing today. Silently she returned to the pickup for the stepladder.

Surprisingly, Kylie and Pam arrived next. Pam irreverently plastered her building permit sticker to the snug curve of jeans across her bottom. Luke had his neatly fastened to his shirt pocket. Cindy defiantly switched hers to match Pam's; she was *not* going to take today too seriously, no matter how grim Luke acted.

At seven o'clock exactly, Luke measured and staked off a square to mark the base of the lighthouse. He tacked together some pieces of plywood he'd brought to use as a form to hold the sand temporarily in place. That was allowable as long as the plywood was removed before the judging. By seven forty-five all the members of the team except Melanie were at work. She rushed up a few minutes later and ducked under the makeshift fence.

"You were supposed to be here at seven," Luke pointed out.

"I know. I'm sorry. But Todd spilled syrup all over the kitchen floor, and then the dog walked in it. And then I realized just at the last minute that I could keep the kids busy and out of my hair all morning by entering them in the children's section. They're down at the other end of the beach constructing a sleeping dog with Howser as a model."

She was out of breath, smiling apologetically, but Luke just handed her a shovel and returned to work before she'd even finished her explanation. *Let him try to get five kids and a dog anywhere on time and see how easy it is,* Cindy thought, annoyed at his brusqueness.

BY MIDMORNING both lighthouse and octopus were taking rough shape. Everything was going nicely. Luke might not be any sand sculpture expert, but he knew organization, efficiency and how to delegate and coordinate responsibility. Pam was on the stepladder sculpting a weather vane bird to decorate the peak of the lighthouse. They were doing the fine detail work from the top down, before the catwalk was carved out. Luke had decided the way to handle the catwalk was to narrow it and to carve sand out beneath it, rather than stick sand to the side of the lighthouse walls, as they had done the night of the practice session. This was going to be done last, because the overhanging catwalk was the part of the sculpture that was the trickiest and the most likely to collapse.

Everything looked good. The octopus arms were evenly matched in size, the head symmetrically bulbous. The sun had burned through the fog, and the coast was at its glorious best. People snapped pictures and called compliments and encouragement. Music blared from a loudspeaker, and the scent of hot dogs and hamburgers hung in the air.

But it wasn't, Cindy thought unhappily, much fun. No clowning, no laughing, no wisecracks or teasing insults. Pam knew lots of people and liked to talk to them, but after Luke snapped at her a couple of times she gave that up. Jet grumbled that he was starving to death but didn't stop to eat. Melanie looked upset when Luke said she wasn't getting the corners of the lighthouse sharp enough. And Luke just scowled whenever Kylie snapped a photo of their work in progress.

"You picked a fine time to cut him off and put him in a mood like this," Pam grumbled to Cindy. This was just after Luke had jumped on Pam for giving the octopus too feminine and cute an expression.

It took Cindy a moment to realize what Pam meant by her tart remark. "But I didn't—I mean—" She broke off, a little embarrassed, although she wasn't quite certain about what. She then started to say that Luke had had some bad news but broke that off, as well. Luke wouldn't like it, even if she didn't give details. But she wasn't certain she cared to apologize for Luke; she resented the way he was taking his job frustrations out on the team. Finally she just smiled and rolled her eyes. "Men," she said, letting Pam make what she would of that indefinite remark.

They finished at a quarter of one. Having the sand dry out and crumble was the biggest danger, and Cindy gave the catwalk another careful wetting with the hand-pumped water sprayer. Some sand castle contests allowed detergent or biodegradable glue to be added to the water, but here they could use only plain water and hope for the best.

Cindy thought their sculpture would be one of the first to be considered by the judges, because their plot was near the head of the double row. But the judges chose to go down the opposite side and work their way back up toward the lighthouse. Luke just stood around looking impatient and grim. Cindy practically held her breath wondering if the catwalk would fall off before the judges arrived.

It didn't. And a few minutes later the announcement of the winners blared over the loudspeaker set up at the judges' stand. The Windy Bunch didn't win fifth place in their division. Or fourth. But they did win third! After that it didn't matter what happened or who came first. Jet grabbed Susan and danced around, and Kylie hoisted Pam on his shoulders for a victory jog around the plot. She was down to her bikini by then, exuberantly waving The Windy Bunch wind sock, and the crowd applauded her as much as the award.

Cindy looked at Luke, uncertain whether to cheer. For all she knew, he might be angry that they hadn't placed first. At the moment she couldn't tell what he was thinking. His face had that old set, guarded expression.

Then, as Kylie came to a halt by Luke, Pam leaned over from her position on Kylie's shoulders and, with an audible smack, kissed Luke on the forehead.

"You're probably the world's worst-tempered king, but you know your stuff. We finally won something!"

Luke just stood there a moment longer, and then he grinned and everybody started shaking hands and hugging and congratulating each other. His high-handed supervision and blunt criticism were forgiven and forgotten now that they had achieved such positive results. Cindy joined in, but she doubted that she felt as exuberant as the others.

A little later one of the judges came around to plant a ribbon and plaque on their sculpture. There was also a hundred-dollar-bill for third prize.

Cindy started gathering up tools. Winning was fine, but she wasn't sure it was better than the haphazard fun they'd had in previous years.

She glanced up when Luke walked over. "Congratulations," she said. "You're the winner."

"It was a team effort." When she didn't say anything he added a little ruefully, "I suppose I may have taken my position as, mmm, king too seriously."

"For a while I thought there might be an insurrection among the troops, but apparently everyone thinks the result was worth the effort."

"But you don't." When she again didn't comment, he said, "I'm sorry if I was a little rough. I guess I just felt the need to prove I wasn't a loser at . . . everything."

Quick sympathy flooded through Cindy, and she mentally kicked herself for her lack of understanding. Of course he'd feel that way! He wasn't callously taking his fury and frustration out on them, as she'd assumed; he had simply felt an overpowering need to prove something about his self-worth to himself. On this particular day winning something, even if it was only a sand sculpture contest, really mattered.

She reached up and kissed him on the mouth. "Congratulations." This time she meant it. Teasingly she added, "We couldn't have done it without your nagging and whip cracking."

"As of right now," he said, "I hereby resign as king." He solemnly took off the cap and handed it to her. She tossed it on the pile of tools.

"Then let's walk around and look at all the other sculptures. There must be a couple of pretty good ones to beat *us*."

They got sandwiches and soft drinks from the ice chest and ate while strolling along the line of sculptures. Jostling crowds of people still milled around, everyone in a holiday mood. Cindy felt that way, too, now.

The sand castles varied from whimsical fairyland creations to imposing Turkish-style structures. A scooped-out cave had intricate cliff dwellings inside. There was a sculptured copy of a famous picture of three horses' heads, a Snoopy surrounded by little bird friends and a motorcycle with driftwood handlebars. It had won a prize.

"Now Jet can say 'I told you so!'" Cindy laughed. "Oh, there's the one that took first place in our division!"

It was a sculpture of two dragons, mother and baby. The sculptors had managed to endow the sand monsters with a touching mother-love sentimentality. The creative detail was marvelous.

"I guess they deserved to win," Luke agreed without envy or regret. He laughed. "Maybe I should have let Pam keep that silly little smirk on our octopus's face."

They went down to the children's section. Melanie's children's project had suffered a disaster. Howser had dug a hole in the reproduction of his ear. However, the children had gotten a Tough Luck award and were happy with it. By the time Luke and Cindy returned to their own lighthouse sculpture, part of the catwalk had collapsed, but everything else was intact. The other team members were gathered there, waiting for them. By now the tide was heading in.

"Hey, it's time to get the party going!" Pam called. "We have a hundred dollars to celebrate with!"

Luke looked at Cindy. He dug in his pocket for the money, but his eyes told her he really didn't feel like whooping it up at some noisy party.

"Maybe we'll join you later. I think we'll just...take things easy for a while," Cindy said. She picked up the plaque and ribbon and handed them to Pam. "Here, take these along for the celebration."

Pam rolled her eyes melodramatically. "Ain't love grand? The lovers have made up and now dey vant to be alone." Unperturbed, she cheerfully grabbed the money from Luke. "We'll be at Max and Joanna's if you feel like joining us later."

When the other team members were gone, Luke said, "As a matter of fact, I do want to be alone. Alone with you, I mean. Not here." His voice suddenly roughened with urgent meaning. He tilted her chin and kissed her. It was a chaste kiss, here among the crowds still wandering around the sand sculptures, but its meaning was patently obvious to Cindy. So was the look of desire in his eyes. Against her lips he added, "I should never have let you leave last night."

His urgency communicated itself to her. She felt it flow through her and return to him, electrified and multiplied in strength. She suddenly needed as much as he did the kind of aloneness she knew he meant. "Let's hurry and finish up here."

They took down the string fence around their sand plot, picked up the litter that had accumulated and checked for tools lost in the sand. Cindy felt a delicious sense of conspiracy and a heightened anticipation as they hurried to escape the crowds. They had a secret, and the secret was that they were going to go home and make love in the middle of the afternoon, while all these people did mundane things like talk and laugh and eat hamburgers.

Yet fate and people seemed joined in conspiracy to delay them. An older man paused to chat about how they'd done the overhanging catwalk. A woman wanted them to pose for a photo. They carried the tools and stepladder back to the pickup and met Max hurrying back. He'd lost a pocketknife in the sand. They hadn't much choice but help him look for it. It was a wasted effort, of course.

By the time they finally got to the pickup, Luke grumbled, "Now all we need is a traffic jam."

They got it, of course. The endless delay frustrated them, and then the frustration made them laugh—a laughter that crackled with the breathless electricity of anticipation.

But at last they were back at Cindy's cottage, alone in the pastel glade of her bedroom, curtains closed against sunlight and intruding sounds. Luke crushed her against him, bending her back in an arch that made her feel more breathless than she already was.

"Did you mind that I rushed you away from the party and everything?" Luke asked.

"Only that you didn't rush a little faster."

He laughed softly, pleased at her eagerness. "I was afraid you might be angry. But I need you so much, sweet Cinnamon. I need you now."

Cindy vaguely understood that part of that need was tangled up with his awful feeling of failure about the job, that even though he knew the rejection was unjust and undeserved, it had stabbed at the very foundations of his manhood. She wanted to tell him he didn't need to prove anything to her, but said nothing. He needed to make love to her in the same way that he'd needed to win the contest at the beach. Yet Cindy didn't mind that part of his need, because it wasn't a need for just any woman; it was a need for her. And she wanted to give him everything he needed.

Yet now that they were alone, he seemed in no hurry. He didn't rush her to bed or tear at her clothes—though she wouldn't have objected if he had.

He removed each item of her clothing slowly, lovingly as she stood in the center of the room, as if he were peeling the wrapping from some mysterious package. T-shirt, jeans, bra, bikini panties. He kissed her as he went, his lips leaving hot, crisscrossed trails across her body. She knew her body was no longer a mystery to him, yet when she was naked he studied it with a fresh delight, as if it was a treasure that he had failed to appreciate fully.

"If there's a . . . a Best Undresser award, you're the winner," she said shakily. He drew a fingertip across her abdomen, and a tremor in the muscle followed his touch.

"What's the prize?"

"Me."

"I must have won the Grand Champion award to deserve such a magnificent prize." He smiled. He leaned over to kiss the uptilted curve of her breast but stopped before he got there to watch with pleasure as the nipple grew rigid with anticipation.

"And another award, for the Man with the Magic Lips," she whispered when his lips finally touched her. His hands clasped her waist and held her steady when she started to sway.

He carried her the few steps to the bed and quickly shed his own clothes. They came together with a passion sweetened by delay and spiced by anticipation, and he made love to her with tender expertise, loving skill. She was aware in some hazy corner of her mind that his lovemaking was less wildly abandoned than it often was. They didn't do the silly, playful things they sometimes did, didn't experiment with the positions that often aroused their laughter as much as their passion.

Today he concentrated on the familiar, the kisses and touches and movements that they knew brought them both to bursting peaks of satisfaction. And he did them all to skillful perfection, to the point where her thoughts and observations faded into oblivion, lost in the whirl of hot stars in her mind. She lost track of the specific messages of her senses, the feeling of skin against hot skin, the sound of whispered love words, the taste of his warm mouth. They all joined together in one feeling that his body was a part of her and she a part of him.

Today she was receiver, not giver, knowing that was the way he wanted and needed it, and she reveled in the lazy glory of being totally in his control. He was master and guide, teacher and commander, and he carried them both along a sensuous journey that wound ever higher in this realm where senses and emotions combined. Dreamily she thought that she couldn't have stopped the glorious trip upward even if she'd wanted to—and she didn't want to, not now, not ever.

Sometimes their peaks came a few moments apart, but this time they were as one, in perfect unison, joined in a double rapture.

Sometime later, Cindy wasn't sure how long she'd drifted in the dreamy aftermath of love, she murmured, "And the Most Magnificent Lover award, too."

He laughed softly and cradled her in his arms, and they both slept.

LUKE WOKE FIRST. He lifted his head, careful not to disturb Cindy, and smiled down at her. Her pale-blond hair haloed her face, and her hand lay on her pillow beside her head, palm trustingly open. A sleeping angel with a half smile on her lips, as if she was having pleasant dreams—and an earthy smudge of sand on her temple.

He let his head settle back on the pillow. He couldn't see the clock, but daylight still filtered through the lightweight draperies. He tried to go back to sleep but couldn't.

He felt oddly restless and unsettled, and was annoyed with himself for it. They'd won something in the sand castle contest. That was no great accomplishment, of course, but it was something. He'd proved he was a satisfactory lover... although knowing that he'd been proving a point with Cindy made him feel more guilty than pleased. She deserved better than that. He smiled again at the thought of all the sweet, silly little awards she'd bestowed on him. She also, he thought unhappily, deserved better than a guy who had no more future than he had.

That was the real crux of the matter, of course. All day he'd determinedly put the previous day out of his mind, but now it was back, multiplied in meaning. Being passed up for that job wasn't a single, isolated failure. Any hope he'd had of getting back into the exciting stock market work he'd loved was permanently and totally ended.

Cindy stirred and shifted to her side. He momentarily held his breath until she settled back to sleep again. He could feel himself sliding into a grim depression, and there was no point in dragging her down with him.

He also didn't really feel like discussing any more of it with her. His feelings for her were strong and growing, and she'd been sweet and understanding, forgiving about his dark mood. But she couldn't *really* understand, of course. She'd never know the gut despair and disappointment of having everything you'd worked and hoped for unfairly taken away from you.

Carefully he eased his arm out from under her. He'd take a walk or drive or something.

Hell, maybe it was time to do more than that. Maybe it was time to get out before he messed up her life, too. He'd traveled light and fast when he'd come here, and he could leave the same way.

9

LUKE SLIPPED INTO HIS CLOTHES and tiptoed silently to the bedroom door. He glanced back, then realized he shouldn't have. Cindy's eyes flew open as if his glance had physically touched her.

"Where are you going?"

He tried to make light of it. "Don't tell me you were just pretending to be asleep again."

She wouldn't let him get by with that easy evasion, of course. She repeated her question.

"I just thought I'd take a walk or drive or something. You go back to sleep."

"Do you want to go to the party now?" she asked.

He answered the question with one flat word, although the simple "No" was hardly sufficient to express how he felt about celebrating.

"I'll come for a walk or drive with you, then."

She was out of bed and dressing in clean shorts and T-shirt before he could think of any persuasive argument to keep her there. They got in his car. She suggested going somewhere to eat, but he wasn't hungry.

"Maybe you should have let me come alone. I'm not in a real... upbeat mood." He suspected it was a gross understatement.

"That's okay. I understand."

"I suppose we could go down to the beach and admire our handiwork again," he suggested.

Cindy glanced at her wrist, but she wasn't wearing her watch. "The tide is probably in by now, but we can take a walk on the beach, anyway."

The crowds and traffic had let up. Apparently many people had left town as soon as the sand sculpture festival was over, but the sidewalks and streets were still much busier than usual. Waiting lines stretched from the doors of a couple of restaurants.

Luke parked the car, and they walked through the town park to get to the beach. A few people still lingered, some sitting on the retaining wall behind the motel, some walking. Sunlight, unobstructed by land, lingered late through the June evening. A couple of boys were trying to fly a purple, diamond-shaped kite, but the erratic wind took it aloft for only a few moments before making it nosedive back to the sand. Luke absentmindedly thought that Cindy could have made it fly even in the irregular gusts, but the boys were too inexperienced.

"One of yours?" Luke asked, nodding toward the kite.

Cindy nodded. "The festival was good for business. I have to work tomorrow," she added.

From this point they still couldn't see the area of beach where the contest had been held. When they could see it, Luke stopped short and stared.

Of course he'd known the sand sculptures were temporary. Of course he'd known the tide would come in and wash them away. Yet seeing the destruction in progress filled him with an impotent fury. He clenched his fists. All that hard work, all the energy and creativity that had gone into making castles and dragons, lighthouse and octopus . . . wasted. Gone.

They walked along the edge of the surf that washed up the long, flat beach. A few of the sculptures on the landward side of the double line of plots were still vaguely recognizable. The remaining tower of a castle crumbled as they passed by. The cave had collapsed, falling in on the cliff houses like some destruction of a miniature civilization. A whale still wore a foolishly cheerful expression on its sandy face, even though half its body had melted away.

On the side closest to the sea, the destruction was even more complete. The winning dragon sculpture was a shapeless lump. The motorcycle was completely gone. All that remained of their lighthouse and octopus was an anonymous pile of sand. Within minutes the sea would take even that.

The sight deepened Luke's depression. He jammed his thumbs into his pants' pockets, and they walked in silence until they reached the area of jumbled driftwood at the far end of the beach. This was where they'd had that first barbecue, when he had known Cindy was trying out her friends on him. Or maybe trying him out on her friends. They sat on a log and looked back toward the scene.

"Looks kind of like a battlefield, doesn't it?" he commented. "Everything destroyed."

"But no real casualties," she pointed out.

Some children pranced and played at the edge of the surf, dashing into the white foam, darting back as if daring it to chase them. They scrambled to the top of a shapeless heap of sand that had once been a graceful sculpture and screamed with delight as the sea washed sand away beneath their feet.

"It's kind of like life on a small scale. You strive and struggle to accomplish something, and then it's all wiped out in a brief period of destruction by relentless forces completely beyond your control, just like the tide washing away the sand sculptures."

Cindy tucked her arm through his. "There's another way to look at it. Everything is washed clean. No matter what mistakes were made or what unfortunate events happened, they're all gone. The slate is clean and fresh, all ready to start over and build on again."

He knew she wasn't talking just about sand sculptures and the beach and tide. She was talking about what had happened to him . . . just as he was. He glanced at her, suddenly angry with her naively optimistic philosophy.

"You can believe that because you've never had everything you've worked for washed away and destroyed—just a sand sculpture that took only a few hours to build. It's easy to be cheerful and upbeat when nothing really bad has ever happened to you. I'm talking about a lifetime of work. I'm talking about a future destroyed."

"You think you're the only one that's ever happened to?" Her voice sounded oddly strained, as if she was trying to hold back anger of her own. "You think I really don't know?"

Her blue eyes looked wintry and remote, yet pitying. Damn it, he didn't want her pity! "You don't need to feel sorry for me," he muttered. "I'm not looking for sympathy."

"If I feel sorry for you . . . and I'm not sure that I do," she added with reflective coolness, "it's not because of the injustice of what happened to you. I'm sorry for you because you aren't rising above it."

"What do you know about rising above anything?" he asked, not bothering to conceal scorn and the bitterness that had eaten away at him for so long. "You're a carefree, lighthearted spirit. You live from day to day. You fly your kites and build your sand castles." He looked at the boys far down the beach. They had their kite up and flying now. "But I can't spend all my life blithely dancing in the wind the way you do."

"And I've never known disappointment or failure or despair. That's what you think?"

"Sure, I suppose you've been disappointed," he granted. "Everyone has been in one way or another. There are always rough places in everyone's life."

"How generous of you to acknowledge that! It's just that *your* disappointment and failure are bigger and more important than anyone else's. The wrong that was done *you* a greater injustice than that done to anyone else!"

Her tone was uncharacteristically mocking, and he looked from the kite in the air back to her again. The way she put it made him feel uncomfortable and self-conscious, perhaps even a little guilty. Yet the feeling didn't take away his anger. He'd warned her that he wasn't exactly prime-time company today. "And I suppose you're now going to tell me about all the people who are worse off than I am."

"No. Now I'm going to tell you about me."

Luke's first instinct was to snap that he knew all about her. Yet as he looked at her he knew that wasn't true. He remembered the times when a bleakness had briefly invaded her eyes, like stars going out in usually sparkling depths. The times he'd suspected that there were layers to her character that he'd never touched. The times she'd lightly passed over some question about the past and deftly led his attention elsewhere.

Luke briefly considered the possible trouble spots in her life. A lack of relationship with her real father? No. The "Invisible Mr. Jones," as Cindy had once called him, was merely a biological fact, not an emotional issue. Her relationship with the man she'd once been in love with? She'd spoken of him with a certain regret but certainly not as if her heart had been broken. Then he knew. "Gymnastics?"

"From the time I was a small child I was dedicated to gymnastics. Everything else was secondary. I missed out on most of the normal activities of children and teenagers, but it wasn't because they were denied me by someone else. It was my choice to miss out on them, because only gymnastics really mattered. And I was good," she added with sudden fierceness. "I had some natural talent—"

"A lot of it, from the little I've seen."

She ignored the interruption. She was walking through memories, and he could see the trail was not an easy one, although the obstacles were not yet clear to him.

"And I was willing to work. I considered everything else merely an annoying or tedious interruption in what I really wanted to do, which was to perfect my skills. I had this private little dream that someday I'd be the first woman to make a perfect score of ten in every women's gymnastics event at the Olympics." Her small smile was private as she looked inward at the dream. He didn't know enough about gymnastics to know whether some other woman had accomplished it.

No wonder she'd recognized him as a workaholic, he thought wryly. Her dedication to gymnastics made his involvement with his job look almost like that of a dilettante.

"I won awards. State, regional, national."

"I should have heard of you." Luke felt embarrassed. He'd realized she was good but not how good. Apologetically he added, "I suppose I just never followed gymnastics much. I'm mostly a football fan."

Luke thought the statement might offend her, but she merely nodded, as if his words confirmed some inner thought. "That's part of what I'm getting at."

Luke found the comment enigmatic, but he didn't ask for explanation. He let her continue.

"At sixteen I was in line to make the Olympic gymnastics team. Everyone, including me, was sure I'd make it. But I injured my knee in a fall from the uneven parallel bars. I had surgery—"

He remembered the faint scars on her knee. "Unsuccessful?"

"No, it was successful. Or it would have been if I'd given it a chance to heal properly. But in my determination to make the Olympic team I started working out too soon. I injured the knee again...and was out of consideration for the Olympics. I wound up watching them on television—from a hospital bed."

"You gave up then?" She gave him a scornful glance, and he quickly answered his own question. "You didn't give up."

"No. I had four years to prepare for the next Olympics, and I was more determined than ever. But my knee kept giving me problems. I had a couple more surgeries. The doctors said I should be able to engage in most normal activities, but they weren't enthusiastic about my continuing with gymnastics. But normal activities weren't what I wanted, of course. My whole world was gymnastics."

"With not much room in it for that hometown boy."

She nodded. "So I kept working and practicing. I won a few more awards, but I couldn't seem to achieve the style I'd had before."

"Because of your knee?"

"Partly. But that wasn't all of it. At fifteen, I was five foot four, already a little tall compared to most top women gymnasts today. And then, horror of horrors, I grew three inches. I thought I already had my full growth, of course, but I shot up like the proverbial weed. And put on weight to match."

"You got fat?" He eyed her slim figure disbelievingly.

"No, not fat. The weight was muscle...and maybe just normal development. My genetic destiny. But at five foot seven and a hundred and thirty pounds, I was larger than most other contestants." She laughed reminiscently and ruefully. "Sometimes, around the smaller girls, I'd feel as big and clumsy as a lumbering hippopotamus among a flock of fleet-footed gazelles. Small size and weight are a distinct advantage, if you'll look at the current champions. I don't mean judges are prejudiced in their favor," she added quickly. "It's just that a smaller, lighter girl may be able to do three movements in the time and air space in which a larger one can do only two. But then, you don't follow gymnastics to notice these things."

He looked at her sharply, wondering if she was being sarcastic or critical, but she wasn't. She was just stating a fact.

Just as matter-of-factly she added, "Lots of other people don't notice, either."

So what was she getting at? "Many people don't care about football, either." He hadn't meant anything in particular by the remark, but she nodded as if he'd just said something profound. She looked at him expectantly, as if she thought he should carry the observation to some further conclusion. None occurred to him, however. Instead he said, "Apparently even nature was against you."

"So it seemed. Anyway, by the time of the next Olympics, I simply failed to make the team. Oh, I had lots of excuses to give myself and others. I'd gained too much weight. I'd lost too much practice time because of the surgeries. My knee still wasn't as strong or flexible as it should have been."

"No doubt true."

"Probably. But it didn't really matter what the reasons were, because it's only the bottom line that counts: I didn't make the team. My coach advised against trying again. I'd be twenty-four by the time the next Olympics came around. There have been some winning twenty-four-year-old gymnasts in the past, of course. Maybe even some hundred-and-thirty pound ones. But it's basically a young girl's sport these days. So there I was, a washed-up has-been at age twenty."

He had to protest that harsh judgment. "You're not—"

She held up a hand to stop him. "The coach said I didn't need to give up gymnastics completely, however. I had a lot to offer as a teacher and coach, he said. He was opening a gymnastics school of his own in Southern California, and he offered me a job."

"I told you the other day that you could teach—"

Again she stopped him. "I took the job. Every day I went in and watched and guided these girls, all so young and eager. And lithe and limber and nimble and bouncy, with limitless futures ahead of them . . . all the things I *wasn't*. The trouble was, I didn't really want to help someone else become a champion. I still wanted to be one myself. I was envious and resentful and all the other unlovely things no one wants to admit to being. I'm ashamed of the way I felt. I was ashamed of it even then. But the feelings were there, and they aren't exactly qualities that contribute to being a good teacher. I knew the coach was going to fire me, and I didn't blame him, so I quit to save him the trouble. So there I was with failure number two."

"You didn't look envious or resentful when you were helping Tracy the other day."

"I know. I felt . . . good. I was really pleased when she managed to do the aerial cartwheel." She sounded bemused.

"How is your knee now? I've seen the scars, but I've never noticed you limping or favoring the knee. And it didn't seem to bother you that night I watched you on the beach."

"It doesn't bother me much anymore, if I don't overdo it. But you're sidetracking me." Determinedly she moved back on course. "So I quit the job at my coach's school. I came to the Oregon coast about the same way you did, because my family had vacationed here one summer and I remembered it as being beautiful and kind of isolated. It seemed as good a place as any to banish myself to, since my life was over, anyway."

Luke laughed in spite of himself. "How melodramatic."

She laughed, too. "Yes, I can see that now. But I couldn't then. I got a job at a Mexican fast-food place."

"And made terrible tacos," he filled in, remembering what she'd once said.

"Yes. Definitely terrible tacos. I wasn't making much money, and that was also my self-sufficient, live-off-the-sea phase. I muddled along. But all the time I felt as if I was living in a kind of shadow world, because the only real world was gymnastics. Accomplishments in that world were the only ones that really mattered. I kept track of who was winning at the various gymnastics meets and watched every gymnastics event that was broadcast on TV—"

"Wasn't that doing the old salt-in-the-wound routine?"

She considered that. "Yes, I suppose it was. It hurt to watch, but it was my window on the real world, because now I was out in the cold, and there wasn't anything out here. Then one afternoon Pam—yes, our same impetuous Pam. She worked at the same place. Her specialty was terrible burritos—asked me to come along on a white water jet-boat ride up the river. I said I couldn't because there was a gymnastics program on TV. She got exasperated with me and said, 'Who *cares*?'"

"So you jumped on the boat and forgot about gymnastics?"

"No, it wasn't that sudden, of course. I wasn't struck with some illuminating bolt of lightning. In fact, at first I was just angry at Pam for making a statement that I considered almost sacrilegious. But I finally began to see that there were lots of people—millions of people, in fact—who couldn't care less about gymnastics. It wasn't the only thing that mattered, except in my own narrow mind. I was finally able to back off and see that, yes, I'd failed in gymnastics, both as participant and teacher. I had no future there. But that didn't mean I was a failure at life, unless I let it do that to me."

"Obviously an important turning point."

"Luke, there are all sorts of worlds existing within our larger world." Her voice was suddenly deadly serious, the rueful, half-amused look at herself gone. "There's the world of gymnastics, in which I revolved. There's the world of football. There are worlds of running and tennis and theater and racing cars and—selling widgets. And sometimes people get so tied up in these little worlds that they forget there's a larger, beautiful world out there, a world that doesn't give a damn about gymnastics or widgets . . . or stocks and bonds and mutual funds."

Until that very moment, as plain as it had been, Luke hadn't realized where she was heading. He had thought she was giving him a roundabout pep talk that would wind up by telling him to try for another job with a different stock brokerage company. And that wasn't what she was saying at all. She was dismissing the whole stock market world as if it was no more than an insubstantial puff of smoke.

His defenses instantly rose. She was drawing parallels between situations that weren't comparable! Granted, gymnastics took skill and talent and hard work, but the field was hardly comparable to the financial marketplace of the nation. Nor was life as simple as a tide-washed stretch of sand, ready to build on again.

"So you found a new world, and you're telling me I should, too." He didn't wait for her response, and in sudden anger he attacked. "There's another way to look at what you've done. It could be that you've taken a cowardly, easy way out instead of persisting. It could be that you're trying to pass yourself off as noble and wise, when in reality you're just plain selfish, not sharing your knowledge and skills with—"

Cindy's eyes flashed. "I'm not saying I'm noble or wise or anything—" She broke off and took a deep, steadying breath. "Neither am I disparaging or belittling the importance of gymnastics or the stock market. I'm simply saying it's a mistake to get totally tied up in *any* small world. Success in the stock market isn't all that matters any more than success in gymnastics is."

She was looking out across the sea now. The sinking sun gilded the gently rolling water with a sheen of gold. She absentmindedly massaged the knee, as if talking about it had brought back the old pain. The slanting angle of sunlight highlighted the barely visible scars, making the thin, white lines glow with a cruel, pearly luster.

Luke's anger and resentment evaporated. He wasn't certain he could accept her casual dismissal of the field he'd once been in, the world he'd tried to rejoin and failed. He wasn't sure accomplishments there weren't more important than success elsewhere. But he knew one thing. He'd been mistaken about her. Her life hadn't been the blithe, ever sunshiny rose garden he'd assumed. He'd been so wrong in his supremely self-centered, arrogant conclusion that she couldn't understand his feelings because she'd never suffered disappointment and failure. His heart reached out to her.

He put his arms around her, and she rested her head against his. They sat that way for long moments, giving and taking in a silent communion of comfort.

"You can add one more award to those you were giving me earlier," he finally said gruffly. "Insensitive Jerk of the Year."

If he expected her to protest, he was wrong. She lifted her head and looked at him, blue eyes guileless. "Sounds good to me," she murmured.

He laughed. He felt something snap inside him, maybe the chain that bound him to that deep pit of depression. "Feel like going to the party now?" he asked.

"Today's lecture is over, so why not?"

They drove out to Max and Joanna's big house. Music spilled from the open doors and windows. When they went inside they found there were considerably more celebrators than team members. Apparently the party was open to anyone. Luke didn't know some of the people who greeted them, but they seemed to know him.

He got "Hey, King" greetings, a "We showed 'em, huh!" and a few friendly insults. Luke grinned back and lifted a hand in greeting here and there. The plaque and ribbon occupied a place of honor over the fireplace. They found beer and chips and followed the scent of meat barbecuing in the backyard. It was a cook-your-own deal. Luke added wieners to the grill for himself and Cindy, and she loaded hot dog buns with all the goodies.

Joanna reported that business at the kite shop had been great that day. "Hey, have you seen the pictures yet?" she added. "Kylie, where're your pictures?"

Kylie had taken his film to the one-hour photo finishing shop in town. Luke shook his head when he saw himself in the photos. He looked like some grim-faced despot bullying the peasants.

"It's a wonder the rest of you didn't bury me under the octopus," he admitted.

"Don't think we didn't consider it," Pam retorted. "But I figured Cindy would just dig you up. She does seem attached to you, although sometimes I can't understand why."

Luke glanced at Cindy. "Yeah, sometimes I wonder, too."

Later, Max and some helpers moved back furniture to make a place for dancing in the living room. One group gathered there, another group sat in the kitchen exchanging tall tales, and Jet kept the charcoal grill going in case anyone wanted more food. Luke suspected there would be no leftovers whenever Jet was around. Kylie took orders for reprints of the photo series. People came and went, drifting from one group to another.

Luke and Cindy went back to the cottage about midnight. They didn't discuss whether they would spend the night together. They just showered together and slipped into the single bed that never seemed too small for the two of them, in spite of its narrowness. They didn't make love again. Luke just held her tenderly and lovingly. He realized she had put pain and unhappiness behind her, but he wished he could somehow change and soften the hard knocks of the past for her.

Yet if he could, perhaps she wouldn't be here in his arms right now. And there was also the hazy thought, half lost in sleep, that if his past had been different, he wouldn't be here now, either.

CINDY WOKE and tiptoed out first the following morning, just barely in time to hurry down to the shop and open up. Joanna brought in the plaque, ribbon and a photo of their prizewinning sculpture for display. The day was busy.

When she got home, she found a note from Luke. It said that he had some things to think about, but he'd see her in a few days. She wasn't upset. She knew this wasn't a rejection of her or of what had been said in their long talk on the beach. He simply had some serious thinking to do about the direction of his career and his life.

And, surprisingly, she realized she also needed time and space to do some thinking along those lines.

WHEN SHE STILL HADN'T HEARD from him by the end of the week she didn't know quite what to think. In her vocabulary, the "few days" were definitely up. Her confidence that he was finding a fresh perspective on his problems turned into worry that he had sunk into some isolated depression. Several times she was on the verge of calling or going over to his apartment, but each time she restrained herself, afraid he'd jump to the conclusion that she thought he wasn't capable of working this out on his own.

On the following Monday morning, her day off, she stood at her kitchen window, eating the crumbs from an ancient box of cold cereal, at the same time berating herself for not preparing and sitting down to a proper meal. Breakfast was definitely more fun when shared. So were most other things. She felt the need for physical activity, but a cold fog that was almost a drizzle discouraged outdoor activity. Not great for the summer tourist business, either, she thought dispiritedly.

She finally decided that she might as well accomplish *something* with the unpromising day and set about the job of cleaning house, doing all the tedious tasks she usually skipped. She turned the mattress before changing sheets on the bed. She scrubbed the tiles in the bathroom. She put drain cleaner down the slow-running sink and fanned the acrid fumes that rose. She cleaned the refrigerator, not investigating the aged leftovers too closely. She had her head in the oven and was scraping some unidentifiable burned offering out of a corner when someone knocked on the door.

"Come in," she called without getting up.

"Don't do it!" he cried.

She leaned back on her heels and eyed Luke warily. "Do what?"

"Aren't you turning on the gas and ending it all? Goodbye, cruel world?"

"Don't be dumb. The stove is electric, and I'm not about to go by baking my head as if it were an eggplant casserole. And why would I turn on the gas and stick my head in the oven if I did have gas?"

"You might at least flatter me by letting me think life without me isn't worth living."

Cindy responded with an unflattering grunt. "I wasn't under the impression that you'd deserted me." She scraped up the blackened cinders from the oven and dumped them in the trash can.

"They make a nice oven cleaner, you know. Spray it on, wipe it off."

"Is that what you came over here for, to tell me how to clean my oven?" she demanded.

"My, aren't we feisty today! Apparently absence has not made the heart grow fonder."

"Luke, where have you *been*? I've been worried." Now that he was here, safe, not depressed or sick and obviously in a jovial mood, she was thoroughly annoyed with him. "You might at least have let me know you were okay."

He grabbed her by the upper arms and kissed her thoroughly if not seductively. "I've missed you."

"There hasn't been much evidence of that. If you've been sending messages by mental telepathy, I haven't been receiving them."

"I've been too busy to send messages, mental or otherwise. Or maybe I didn't want to talk about something and jinx its happening."

He sat on a kitchen chair and pulled her into his lap. He'd had a haircut since she'd last seen him. He was freshly shaved and smelled faintly of pine-scented soap. His thighs made a muscular cushion beneath her. An air of leashed excitement clung to him.

"And what have you been so busy doing?"

"First I did a lot of thinking. Wasn't that what you wanted me to do? Get my head on straight and start looking forward instead of backward?"

"Luke, if you've done something drastic like decide to—to run off and become a male stripper, just tell me. I've had about all the suspense I can stand during this past week."

"Hmm. I'd never considered that particular option. Do you think I have the necessary talent and equipment and all that?"

"Luke—" she began warningly.

"Okay, okay, don't head for the ears," he said hastily. "I have a new job. One in which I'll keep my clothes on."

She sat up straighter. "A new job? You're leaving?"

"No, the job is here. Well, kind of here and kind of not. What I mean is, the company headquarters are in Portland, but they've opened a branch office here. I'll spend some time here, some in Portland and do some other traveling."

"What kind of position is it?"

"I'm the financial manager for Winds Unlimited, the company that's going to put up the wind turbines and do something useful with all that wind energy that goes to waste around here. I've always thought it ought to be good for something more than flying kites. I don't know a *lot* about wind power, but I do know a little because energy stocks were my specialty."

She ignored the teasing jibe about the importance of kite flying. "Luke, I'm . . . astonished. Speechless. That's wonderful! You've started work? That's why I haven't seen you? When will they start building the wind turbines? Why do you have to travel?"

He grinned at the shower of questions. "This is speechless?" he teased. She pinched him warningly on the earlobe, and he hurried on. "First, the actual start of construction date isn't set yet. They're still finishing up some studies to be sure it's all done in the best possible way to protect the environment. I'll do some traveling, because part of my job will be working with investors. And no, I haven't actually started work yet. They're supposed to notify me in a few days of the exact date. I'll probably start work in two or three weeks."

"Why the delay?"

"I want to give a week's notice at the mill, of course." He hesitated momentarily. "But putting off the starting date was their decision, actually."

Cindy didn't want to say anything discouraging, but she couldn't help a twinge of worry. "Does the delay mean anything?" she asked tentatively. "Are they still checking references or something?"

"I laid it all out for them, including what kind of recommendation they'd get on me from Marianna Funds. I think they accepted it at face value. They appear to be an energetic, forward-looking company. They seem more interested in my management abilities and experience dealing with investors." He hesitated again. "But until I'm on the payroll, of course, there is the possibility the job could fall through. I haven't given my notice at the mill yet."

"Well, I'm sure it won't fall through," Cindy said firmly, working to convince herself as much as him. She was at least partly responsible for this, and she didn't like to visualize what might happen to his future or to their relationship if things went wrong again. She could see that he was trying to be optimistic, but his old wariness and distrust weren't gone.

"And so what have you been doing while I've been out restructuring my life?" he asked. She could see that he was determinedly putting aside ominous possibilities about the job.

"Thinking."

He started to say something teasing, then realized she was serious. He pulled her closer to him. "Look, I know things between us haven't exactly been ideal, but when I get my own life straightened out—"

"I wasn't thinking about us, at least not all the time." She pushed his arms aside and stood up. "I've been thinking about what you said about my being cowardly and selfish—"

"Cindy, forget that." He pulled her back to him. "I was angry. I knew what you were telling me was right, even though I didn't want to accept it, and I struck back unfairly."

"No, I think you were right, partly, anyway. At least what you said made me take a long, hard look at myself. I don't think my decision to step out of competition was wrong or cowardly. Neither was making a new life for myself outside gymnastics. But since then I've avoided any involvement with gymnastics, as if I was afraid of it, as if I thought it might reach out and grab me and destroy the balance I've found in my life. Now I realize I don't have to avoid gymnastics and sneak down to the beach to perform as if I were doing something not quite nice."

"Actually, I thought it was quite nice," he said with a smile.

"I also realized I have been selfish. I do have something to share with others who might like to learn." She took a deep breath and plunged in. Until that very moment she'd only been thinking about the possibility of doing this. Now she made the full commitment to herself. "I've decided I'd like to start teaching some gymnastics classes for children."

"Cindy, that's terrific!"

"Of course there are about a million problems involved." She threaded her fingers together and paced the small kitchen.

"How deeply are you planning to get into this? Quit your job at the kite shop?"

She shook her head firmly. "No. I'll just have evening classes a few nights a week. Steller Beach isn't large enough to support a full-time school. And I don't think I'd want to get into it that extensively," she added thoughtfully. She smiled and added, "Peculiar as it may seem to you, I really do enjoy my job at the kite shop. And kites have their place in the world, too."

"So what are all these big problems?"

"I'll have to find a suitable place to hold classes, of course. Gymnastics isn't something that can be taught in a spare bedroom. And practicing on beach sand is *not* recommended. I'll need equipment. And students. Perhaps I'll find there aren't all that many children who are interested. Much as I'd like to give lessons for free, I won't be able to because of the expenses involved."

"Those don't sound like a million problems to me. I'll help. And we both know one little girl who'll jump at the chance to take lessons from you. What kind of equipment do you need?"

"Oh!" She pressed her fingertips together and looked out the window, although she wasn't seeing the gloomy drizzle. She was picturing the lavishly equipped schools where she'd trained and worked before. "What I really need is a spring-loaded floor—"

"What's that?"

"It's a floor especially built for gymnastics, with padding and springs underneath. But I know that's out of the question. I'm sure it would cost thousands of dollars." Actually, she had never given much thought to the cost of gymnastics equipment. She had always just used it as if by natural right. "But mats over a regular floor are an absolute necessity. Nothing can be done without them. I prefer hand spotting, so I won't need any of the complicated spotting equipment—"

Luke shook his head. "Lady, you just lost me again. What are you talking about?"

"Hand spotting simply means using just your hands to help the gymnast go through the movements and avoid injury and falls. The spotter helps the performer go into the air at the right time and land safely. Methods other than hand spotting involve using a belt attached to the gymnast, plus various ropes and pulleys. But as I said, I won't need that equipment."

"Okay. What do you need?"

"A balance beam, adjustable height, of course. Uneven parallel bars. A horse—"

"A *horse*?" he cut in doubtfully.

"The inanimate kind you vault over. Not the kind you ride." She laughed. "My, your knowledge of gymnastics is skimpy, isn't it?"

"But I'm willing to learn."

Cindy felt her excitement growing as they talked. She hadn't been on a balance beam or uneven parallel bars since leaving the training school, and she fairly itched to get back on them.

That, however, raised a sobering thought. Was she doing this because she honestly wanted to teach and help others—or for herself? Would those same shameful feelings of envy and resentment toward her young pupils erupt again? Cindy stopped short.

"What's wrong?" Luke asked.

"What if I'm a terrible teacher, as I was before? What if I fail again?"

He stood up and rested his forearms on her shoulders, hands clasped behind her neck. "I could assure you that you won't fail. I could assure you that everything will be fine and there's nothing to worry about. But we both know that isn't true. Everything you try has some risk of failure in it. But you have the skill and experience to be a good teacher, and I think you also have the maturity to handle your own emotions."

"Flattery will get you everywhere," she whispered a bit shakily. His confidence reassured her emotionally, but she felt an odd physical weakness, as if her knees might melt into her ankles. But maybe that had more to do with his nearness than with qualms about her plans. It seemed as if they'd been apart much longer than a week.

He kissed her, differently than the first time. This kiss was long and slow and deep, and his arms held her close to his heart. She returned the kiss with the same tender passion, feeling both physical desire and an outpouring of love. His tongue filled her mouth, and she met it, not with the playful teasing they sometimes shared, but with a sense of deeply intimate union.

His hands slipped lower, to curves that welcomed the familiar caress. She explored the back of his neck with her fingertips, not for the newness of discovery but for the wonder of rediscovery. The solid knob at the nape was still there; so were the familiar cords that were too often tense. She massaged them now, and he lifted his mouth from hers and tilted his head back, eyes still closed.

He groaned lightly, and she felt a little shiver of desire run through him. Then he thrust her away and held her firmly at arm's length.

"Enough of *that*." The dark depths of his eyes didn't agree with the statement, but he still held her away from him.

She wrapped her hands around the strong wrists that held her at arm's length and rubbed the thundering pulse points with her thumbs. She brushed her cheek against his hard knuckles.

"We have things to do," he muttered. He sounded as if he was having difficulty remembering what they were.

"Such as?" she murmured. She lifted his hand and lightly bit the tip of his little finger.

"Do you do this to all the men who come to give you advice about cleaning your oven?" he demanded severely.

Only the ones I'm in love with, she answered silently. Aloud she sighed theatrically. "Very well, since you apparently can't be tempted this afternoon—"

The grip tightened on her shoulders, and he narrowed the distance between them. Warningly he said, "You tempt me."

She smiled and airily extracted herself from his grip. "Just what *are* these terribly important things we have to do?"

"Why, start looking for a suitable place for your gymnastics classes, of course. I really do want to help you get started," he added.

Her heart brimmed with love. He could have carted her off to bed for his own sensuous pleasure—she was willing—but lovemaking wasn't all he wanted to do with her. "If Pam ever buries you in the sand, I really will come dig you up," she promised.

He laughed, kissed her on the nose, then grew serious. "There's one more thing you'd better consider. Given the remarkable propensity of people to sue these days, you'll need liability insurance."

Another sobering thought that she hadn't considered till now, making her realize just how valuable Luke's help could be. She knew gymnastics, but finances or setting up what was actually a small business, part-time though it might be, were definitely not her area of expertise.

She abandoned the housecleaning in mid-oven scraping. Cinders in the oven were not like strange life forms growing in the back of the refrigerator, she rationalized; they weren't going to creep out and envelop the kitchen in blue fuzz. She cheerfully slammed the oven door on them.

Steller Beach had only a small weekly newspaper, and there were no studio spaces listed in the classified ads that sounded suitable for gymnastics classes. So they drove slowly around town in Luke's car, investigating buildings on the side streets.

They found roomy floor space over a garage, but the ceiling was too low. A drafty old warehouse had space enough for a half-dozen classes, plus a ceiling that disappeared in shadows, but the price demanded a more lucrative source of income than a few gymnastics classes would provide. That fact reminded Cindy that she was going to have to work out the economics of her project very carefully.

THE NEXT DAY she called a Portland firm to ask about mats and equipment, and the prices shocked her. She and Luke sat down that evening and on paper worked through various scenarios with the figures. They were almost overwhelming. Starting a gymnastics class was not simple, not like getting a few little girls together to learn basket weaving.

It appeared, she realized unhappily, that the project might collapse before it ever got started.

10

CINDY'S HOPES LIFTED when Luke suggested the town's parks and recreation department might be interested in offering classes. The next day she went into city hall and discussed it with an official. He was interested but said regretfully that because of budget problems, the recreation department was cutting back on its already limited services. Another dead end.

The only encouraging response came from Melanie. She gleefully shouted "Yes!" when Cindy, after rather self-consciously listing her qualifications as a gymnastics instructor, asked if Melanie would be interested in sending Tracy to an evening class. "Then I could tell Tracy, 'No, dear, you must *not* do handstands on the deck railing or cartwheels on the garage roof. Save that for class.'"

Melanie also spread the word that Cindy was planning to teach classes, and mothers of three other little girls called. When Cindy mentioned her problem finding a place to hold the classes, one of the mothers came up with an interesting suggestion. Cindy and Luke followed up on it after she got off work the following afternoon.

The health club that the woman had mentioned was located on a side street behind Steller Beach's small fire department. Cindy knew of its existence. Several people she knew had memberships so that they could use the indoor pool, but Cindy had never been there.

Now she was surprised to find that the clean, friendly club had a good selection of workout equipment as well as the pool. What was more important, it had an unfinished, high-ceilinged room that was being used only three evenings a week by a karate group. The health club would be delighted to rent it out for any or all of the other evenings at a very reasonable fee.

The project was now beginning to look more manageable, for which Cindy was grateful. She was excited enough to want to reserve the space immediately, but Luke prudently advised that she first do a bit of market research.

"Market research!" Cindy echoed, instantly intimidated by the business terminology. She didn't want to open a big training academy; she just wanted to share her skill and knowledge with a few interested children!

Luke laughed and then explained that all he meant was that she should do some test advertising and see how much interest that generated. She made up posters and ran an ad in the weekly newspaper saying that classes were forming. The response pleased her. Mothers of a dozen children aged five to ten, the ages Cindy had specified, definitely wanted their children to participate. The numbers were enough to encourage her, not enough to overwhelm her.

Cindy took the leap and signed a short-term agreement to use the space at the health club two evenings a week. She found some affordable used mats in Portland but postponed buying the other equipment. Tumbling skills and basic floor work came first, and it would be some time before her students progressed to the point of needing balance beam, vaulting horse and bars.

Postponing buying the equipment also eased her apprehensions about herself. She had been afraid that she wanted the classes only because she would then have the equipment to work out on, that she was doing this for her own selfish reasons, not because she wanted to help the students. She was pleased to find this wasn't true, that she was eager to teach even though she wouldn't immediately have equipment available for her own use.

Cindy was so wrapped up in her project that it came as a small shock when Luke announced a few days later that he'd just put in his last shift at the mill. They were at the Chowder House for lunch.

"Monday I become financial manager for Winds Unlimited. I'm a little nervous," he admitted.

"They should realize how lucky they are to get you."

He grinned his thanks at her staunchly loyal support.

"It probably won't be long before you're known as . . . oh, the wind baron of the western world," she teased lightly.

"Unless I qualify for another less exalted term."

"Such as?"

"Unemployed." He saw her quick frown and reached over to cover her hand with his. He smiled reassuringly. "Don't worry. I'm not going gloom and doom on you again. The company has big plans for expansion into other areas of Oregon and Washington if this first project is successful. But it's a new company, and there are risks involved. Wind energy is an old, old source of power, of course. Who knows how far back in history windmills go? But using wind power to produce electricity on a commercial scale is relatively new, and the technology extremely complex. I always warn potential investors of the risks. The whole project could fail."

"And then what? What about *you* if the company fails?"

"Then I pick myself up and start over again. I'd be disappointed and discouraged, of course, but it wouldn't devastate me. I've finally been able to separate an incidence of failure from *being* a failure. And I have no intention of getting so tied up in the world of wind power that I'm . . . blown away by it."

Cindy squeezed his hand, relieved to see that he had things in perspective. "With a pun like that, I'm not sure you don't deserve to be blown away."

"I have to be out of town next week," he added.

"So soon?"

"There are several different types of wind turbines on the market, and I'm going down to California with a couple of company officials to look at the models that are actually in use on some wind farms there. But I'm hoping you and I can do something first, something I've been thinking about for quite a while." His voice held a meaningful warmth and invitation.

For a moment Cindy had the wild thought that he wanted to rush off to Reno and get married immediately, before he started the job. Oregon had a three-day waiting period, but Nevada didn't—

Then she realized he was talking about something else.

"If you could get time off from the kite shop, we'd go away somewhere this weekend. Just the two of us, with no interruptions or distractions...." He lifted his hand and touched her cheek in a gesture that said more than words. "We've never done that, you know."

Cindy's disappointment was momentary, as fleeting as a puff of smoke on the wind, but apparently he caught a whiff of it.

"You don't want to?" he asked. His hand dropped.

"Of course I do!" She grabbed his hand and pressed it to her cheek again. "I was just thinking about...where we might go. We could drive up the coast—"

"No beaches," he said decisively. "No sand, no clams, no kites, no wind. I'll make all the arrangements. You just get the time off."

Cindy felt a little guilty asking Joanna to take over again, but Joanna accepted the request serenely. "I'm saving up all these favors you owe me, and I'm going to spend them when the baby comes." Cindy laughed and agreed.

When they left Steller Beach in Luke's car shortly after noon on Friday, Cindy still didn't know where they were going. On Luke's instructions, she'd packed swim suit and shorts, jeans and jogging shoes, lacy lingerie and a nightgown.

"I can think of all sorts of fun-and-games possibilities with that wardrobe," Cindy mused. Luke just laughed. The gleam in his eyes said he had a few ideas of his own.

The possibilities increased when they arrived in Portland and he took her shopping for a new dress and high-heeled sandals. He chose the dress. It was a sensuous combination of satin and velvet in lighter and darker shades of peach, the style simple to accommodate the lush fabrics. The shoes were barely-there straps that showed off her slim ankles.

Until then, Cindy had assumed they were going somewhere isolated, perhaps some rugged mountain lodge in the Cascades, but this dress hardly seemed appropriate attire for roughing it. Now she was puzzled, and she was even more intrigued when he drove to the airport and unloaded their luggage.

Luke insisted on going alone to the check-in counter. When their flight was called, she finally found out where they were going.

"San Francisco!" she cried in surprised delight.

THEY LANDED in a romantic twilight of city lights. Luke had a rental car waiting. He helped her into it with a gallant flourish. Cindy was lost in the strange city almost before they left the airport, but Luke drove to their hotel with confidence.

He had cautioned her not to eat on the plane, and she was glad she hadn't when they went to a late dinner in the hotel's luxurious dining room. Luke even had their meal already planned, succulent quail stuffed with veal and fresh herbs, a vintage wine that even her inexperienced palate could tell was out of the ordinary and a rich and airy crème de cacao mousse for dessert.

She thought they'd go dancing then, but he surprised her again by taking her for a midnight swim in the hotel's indoor pool. It was built to simulate a tropical paradise, and they frolicked among the hidden rocky grottos and under the waterfall. Then they went back to their room and shed their swimsuits for a more intimate plunge into their own private hot tub. And they made love, of course, slowly and dreamily, drawing out the pleasure until Cindy felt suffused with the sweetness of it.

Room service delivered breakfast at a lazy hour the next morning, and then they went forth to explore Chinatown and ride the cable cars. They had their portraits sketched with astonishing speed and accuracy by a sidewalk artist. They drove up Telegraph Hill and marveled at the view from the top of Coit Tower, incongruously shaped like a giant fire-hose nozzle.

In the evening they saw a flamboyant live musical and ate another luxurious late dinner. By this time Cindy was having some small misgivings about what all this was costing. With a laugh, Luke reassured her.

"I couldn't afford a week of it, that's for sure," he admitted. "But for one special weekend with one special lady, the sky's the limit."

They went dancing, and when they returned to their hotel room, Luke stripped the satin and velvet gown from her body as slowly and sensuously as if he were peeling a ripe peach. He kissed her body as he went, nibbling the firm, glowing skin, teasing her breasts to nearly bursting peaks of longing, and then fulfilling her wildest, erotic fantasies with his love-making.

It was a marvelous weekend, sensually uninhibited. There was no mention of work, his or hers. If she let her imagination drift, she could almost imagine they were on a honeymoon.

But in spite of all the fun and luxury and loving, Cindy was troubled at odd moments by an uneasy sense of finality. It was almost as if they were wrapping up a chapter of their relationship, and Luke was determined to end it on a high note. She kept wondering what he was going to say at the end of the weekend. For a time she'd thought perhaps all this was preliminary to a marriage proposal, but now she suspected thoughts of marriage were only in her mind, not his.

"Thanks, sweet Cinnamon," he might say fondly. "It's been great. But I'm going to be really busy from now on, so . . ." She filled in various endings, none of them happy because they were all variations of a single theme: "So I won't have time to see you as often from now on."

"So I think we should remember the good times and call our relationship quits."

"So I've decided to move to Portland to be closer to company headquarters, and I'll see you around."

When they got back to Steller Beach late Sunday afternoon, what he said was, "Now I have one more request."

"Yes?"

"Will you go down to the beach with me and perform in the moonlight just like you did that night I saw you before we met?"

"The room at the health club is a much better place," she protested. "You can watch me there sometime—"

"No. On the beach in the moonlight. Just you and me." He smiled in the way that made her think that if he asked her to fly, she'd probably flap her arms and try to do it. "Humor me."

They went to the secluded beach where he'd first seen her. Clouds scudded across the moon, sending shadows darting across the restless sea and damp sand. The shifting light made her uneasy, as if it emphasized a certain lack of solidarity about their relationship.

She didn't think she gave her best performance, but Luke's praise was lavish and loving. They went back to the cottage and made love once more. And again, in spite of his tenderness, she was troubled by that disturbing "last time" feeling, as if she should preserve each moment like some precious jewel because it might never come again.

Yet he said nothing. When she tentatively expressed her feeling of uneasiness as they lay warm and damp in each other's arms after making love, he laughed softly at her fears.

"Of course these aren't last times. This is a time of new beginning for me. For us. But we're going to be separated more now than we have been, and I just wanted a very special time for us both to remember and carry with us."

NEXT MORNING, when she watched from the kitchen window as his car backed out of her driveway, Cindy told herself she was being foolish. Everything was going fine for both of them. The weekend had indeed been magically memorable. He had seemed preoccupied when he'd kissed her goodbye, had said his plans were somewhat up in the air for the next few days, but the kiss had still been tender and loving. Every relationship moved into a new phase occasionally, she reminded herself, and that was simply the situation here.

YET THE NEXT FEW WEEKS did nothing to dispel her vague feeling of apprehension. Sometimes she wondered if their relationship, rather than moving ahead or coming to a clearly defined end, wouldn't just gradually fade away, like some kite set adrift in the skies.

They had so little time together! They were always on the run and never in the same direction.

Once Cindy's class started, more children wanted to join, too many to handle in one class. She split the group into two sections divided by age and ran two one-hour classes, one after the other, on Tuesdays and Thursdays. Little Tracy was making almost phenomenally rapid progress. Joanna experienced some later than usual nausea problems with her pregnancy and temporarily couldn't work, and Cindy repaid Joanna's past help by working almost three weeks without a day off at the kite shop. Between teaching classes and handling the kite shop, she was always on the go.

Luke was just as busy. He spent time at both the local and Portland offices and had meetings from Seattle to Los Angeles with potential investors. Being financial manager of Winds Unlimited was not a nine-to-five job, at least not the way Luke handled the position. Cindy sometimes suspected that he was slipping all too readily into the workaholic ways he'd admitted to having before. Once a workaholic, always a workaholic?

Sometimes she wondered if she wasn't doing the same thing. The local newspaper did a very complimentary article on her, and she now had more students than she could comfortably handle in two classes. Others were clamoring for her to start a third class so that they could also join.

Yet Cindy and Luke were both careful not to use their limited time together to complain or accuse or argue. They shared a togetherness and some whimsical private jokes about their mutual involvement with wind power. Others might complain about the wind, but they rejoiced in it, because it was vital to both of them. Once, when the fog lay heavy over the windless coast for almost a week, they went down to the beach and solemnly held a little wind dance ceremony. And the very next day the wind blew!

Luke came by to watch her classes a couple of times. Once he asked, "How do you feel about the kids now? Does it hurt to watch them?"

She shook her head. "It's been a little like meeting an old, lost love again and finding that you can now be good friends. All the anger and envy are gone. I enjoy the children's triumphs—" A little girl practicing a handstand tumbled to the side for the third time and sat there with tears rolling down her face. "And sympathize with their failures," she added with a smile before going to help the girl keep her balance for a few moments.

Luke kept saying that his work load would slack off before long. Cindy said hers should, too, as the slower fall and winter months approached.

Yet so far nothing like that showed signs of happening, and they were both still running at breakneck pace.

On a rare full Friday evening together, they had a private little celebration in the new apartment Luke had just moved into. It had an ocean view, fireplaces in living room and bedroom, redwood deck, dishwasher...and a king-size bed that looked implausibly enormous after the singles they'd shared. The rainbow kite Cindy had once given him decorated a living-room wall.

For this special occasion Cindy wore high heels and the peach dress Luke had bought her. She hadn't had occasion to wear either since the San Francisco trip. Luke unplugged the telephone, because the people at Winds Unlimited were prone to call at all hours. They built fires in both fireplaces. They cooked dinner in the lovely new kitchen and ate by flickering firelight. Luke opened a bottle of champagne with a flourish, and they laughingly...if none too accurately... lifted delicate glasses to each other's lips.

Luke didn't have a stereo yet, but they searched the radio dial until they found romantic music. They danced on the redwood deck, unmindful of the cool, foggy mist swirling around them, conscious only of the warmth in each other's arms.

Then they went back inside to make love in that huge new bed for the very first time. They laughed in delight at all that delicious space and used every inch of it with wild abandon. Cindy had thought they had already reached the topmost heights of making love, but this time they found exciting new peaks . . . and lazy, lovely little valleys and byways, as well.

Afterward Cindy snuggled into the familiar, warm cave of Luke's body that curved around her. She liked the enormous new bed, but at times like this she knew it would never really matter to her if they had only a cot to share.

"Now I want to talk," Luke announced. He was still holding her close, but his voice was firm and nonsnuggly.

"We had all evening to talk," Cindy protested sleepily. She squirmed more deeply into the warm cave. She was pleasantly satiated with food and love, too content for conversation. Luke's chest against her back, his arms around her and his hand on her breast were all she wanted.

"But I wanted to catch you in a special moment when you're feeling all warm and mellow and receptive," he murmured.

"You mean you plied me with breast of chicken and champagne and lovemaking for some ulterior motive?"

He nuzzled her ear with his lips. "Only if you consider love an ulterior motive."

She looked back over her shoulder at him. The broader width of his shoulders loomed over her. The fireplace was behind him, and she could see only the silhouette of his head in the dim light from the dying embers; his features were hidden in shadow.

"I want to ask you something."

The vague uneasiness about their relationship that had dogged her for weeks had melted away on this special evening. It had been a marvelous time, relaxed, comfortable. They'd shared dining and dancing, laughter and companionship and intimacy. She had never felt closer to him. He must feel the same way, she realized. He must feel as she did, that it was finally time to carry their relationship to a deeper commitment.

But it is not polite, she reminded herself with an inner smile, *to shout "Yes!" even before the man proposes.* So she turned over, rearranged herself in the embrace of his arms and legs, and phrased the word as an encouraging question. "Yes?"

"We are two very busy people who love each other. Right?"

"Right."

"When I am coming, you are usually going. And vice versa. Sometimes it seems as if we barely get within waving distance. And I want to be much closer than that."

"It's hard to snuggle up to a long-distance wave," Cindy agreed.

"What I'm suggesting wouldn't change the fact that we're often running in opposite directions, but it would give us the same base of operations so we might at least run into each other a little more often. And we wouldn't have as many of those wasted times when we could have been together but weren't because our signals got crossed."

That had happened more than once. He'd get in late from working a day or two in Portland, not call the cottage because he figured she was already asleep, and then discover she'd been waiting up for him. Or she'd come home from class, call him, think that no answer meant he'd stayed in Portland, and go to bed. Then they'd figure out later that he'd merely been in the shower when she'd called.

So she knew what he meant. If they were married they wouldn't get their signals crossed so often. They'd be together every possible minute that their busy schedules allowed. But what she said with teasing tartness was, "You want us to hire a full-time traffic coordinator?"

He touched her lips with a fingertip, and she could feel the warmth of his smile even in the darkness. "No, sweet Cinnamon, I want you to come live with me. I didn't buy this football-field-size bed because I wanted all this space to sleep in alone."

Cindy swallowed, glad she hadn't given away the fact that she had thought he had marriage in mind. So she'd been mistaken again. He wasn't proposing marriage, just living together.

She murmured a hazy "Umm" to give herself time to think. She loved Luke. Deep down, to her love meant the total and permanent commitment of marriage. Yet even though she was momentarily a bit disappointed with his suggestion, she wasn't necessarily opposed to the idea of living together. She knew of such situations that had led to happy marriages; she knew equally promising relationships that had fizzled in the living-together stage. The arrangement posed certain risks, but so did marriage or any other worthwhile endeavor. For the two of them, she reflected, living together could be a sensible, nonimpulsive way to deepen their relationship without rushing too soon into marriage . . . if it meant the same thing to both of them.

She put the question thoughtfully. "Do you look on living together as a step toward marriage or an alternative to it?"

"I'm sure we'd want to consider marriage eventually." Luke hesitated a moment and then asked, "Are you angry because I didn't suggest that we get married immediately?"

"No, not angry. Although I suppose I do wonder why you prefer this . . . other status."

He rolled over on his back. The profile of his face against the dim firelight faced the ceiling. His throat moved in a rough swallow, as if he'd perhaps rather not say what he was thinking.

Finally he did say it. "Cindy, I love you. It took me quite a while to admit that to myself, because admitting it raised all sorts of questions about the future. If I once admitted it to myself, I knew I'd have to so something about it, and that wasn't a problem I wanted to face."

"I see." Cindy carefully kept the words noncommittal, nonhostile, yet a certain resistance stirred and stiffened inside her. It was a little disconcerting to realize that he felt their love was a "problem." "So now that you've faced the problem, your solution is that we should live together."

"You don't sound wildly enthusiastic."

"I haven't rejected the idea."

"Are you worried that I'm still a workaholic? Do you think I'm so wrapped up in this new job that I won't have time for us?"

"I don't see you taking much time out for fun," she admitted. "You never have flown that kite I gave you."

"I must be the only man in the world who gets nagged at because he won't go fly a kite." Luke sounded more amused than annoyed, however. He turned on his side again and kissed her on the nose. "Between working at the kite store and holding gymnastics classes, you aren't taking much time out for fun, either."

"Yes, that's true. Are you saying you prefer living together to marriage because *I'm* too involved with my work?"

"No! Of course not. I'm proud of you. I just want us to be together as much as we can."

"But you still haven't explained why you prefer living together to marriage."

He flopped over on his back again and crossed his hands behind his head. She was aware of the small, uncharacteristic gap between their bodies. The air in the gap felt cold against her love-warmed skin, and she had the uneasy feeling that he didn't like her persistence in seeking an answer to that particular question.

"Cindy, I do love you," he repeated. "But marriage is a lifetime trust and commitment that I just don't feel I can make yet." He sounded defensive, perhaps even a mite guilty. But not in the least uncertain. This was obviously not an impulsive action; he'd thought about it long and seriously.

Cindy's first bristly thought was, why couldn't he make the full, lifetime commitment of trust? Although she was willing to live with him, or had been until this unexpected statement jarred her, she was also capable of making a marriage commitment. Why wasn't he?

The answer was disconcertingly obvious. He had worked through his career problems. He had recaptured his self-confidence and was charging ahead. He had accepted her philosophy about keeping a proper perspective on the importance of small worlds in the total world around him. But nothing had changed in his feelings about *people*. He was perhaps better now at concealing his wariness and suspicion than when she'd first met him, but his basic feelings of distrust were still there . . . feelings that included her.

"I'm sure you can understand why," he added after silent moments had slipped by.

"So you thought you'd put me on probation for a while. See if I work out satisfactorily." She couldn't keep a certain hostility out of her voice. All the good feelings of the evening seemed to be draining away, taking all the tenderness and leaving a precarious politeness.

"I just don't feel ready to jump into marriage! Is that so difficult to understand? I love you—" He said the three words almost angrily, as if he resented having to repeat them.

"I'm not certain love and trust can be separated, as you seem to be doing. I get the feeling you not only distrust marriage but lack trust in me, as well. I think that's something we have to work out before we make any decisions."

The fire hissed and flared briefly as some of the dying embers fell together. Luke still stared at the ceiling. She waited, hoping he'd deny what she'd just said about his not trusting her.

"It's not exactly a lack of trust," he protested finally. "But experience is a pretty rough teacher, and I learned some hard lessons about depending on people."

"I know you did, but I'm not one of your fair-weather business associates who disappears when the going gets rough! Luke, I love you."

"But you don't want to live with me."

"It isn't that simple—"

"You won't be convinced I love you unless we get married."

He made it sound like an accusation, and it took all her willpower not to snap back at him. She finally managed to say in a fairly neutral tone, "At this point I think we should simply go on the way we have been."

"You know all the reasons why that isn't satisfactory." Luke sounded impatient. Then he abruptly stopped speaking, and she could almost feel the vibrations of his silent thoughts. Finally he said stiffly, "Very well, if you're really opposed to living together and insist on marriage, I suppose I can go along with that. How soon would you like to do it?"

She sat up in bed and looked at him, appalled by his implication that he was willing to get married but only because she was pressuring him. How could he possibly think she was so shallow and manipulative that she'd try to force him into marriage! His words made her feel hurt, angry, humiliated. They downgraded her love for him.

"I'm not insisting on anything! And I don't appreciate your attitude that marrying me would mean some . . . some big sacrifice on your part!"

"I didn't mean to imply that." But the stiffness was still in his voice and in his back, as well, as he sat in bed beside her. "But if living together isn't acceptable to you and marriage is—"

"Luke, love isn't like some business deal where you can make offer A, and if that doesn't work then you come up with alternative B!"

"I think you're oversimplifying—"

"Apparently I haven't expressed my feelings simply enough! I'm saying no to both marriage and living together."

He silently mulled over her angry statement, then asked, "Do you care to offer some explanation? I've been under the impression that you were in love with me, but perhaps, just because you've been saying it, I jumped to the mistaken conclusion that it was true."

There it was, the old suspicion, the old distrust now out in the open. He'd been betrayed by friends; they'd said things they hadn't meant. He'd lost trust in them, and now he wouldn't trust her and her love, either.

"Apparently I've had some mistaken impressions, too," she retorted angrily.

"About what?" he asked.

"About thinking you'd changed."

"You think I'm devoting too much time and investing too much of myself in this new job?"

Yes, she had some apprehensions along those lines. In recent weeks he had given every indication of slipping back into a totally work-centered life. But that wasn't her deepest worry. She yanked the sheet to her chest in frustration. Apparently nothing she had said had gotten through to him.

"I'm beginning to think your mind is so full of thoughts about wind turbines and expenses and profits and investors that there isn't room for changing your fixed attitudes about not trusting people—including me!"

"Cindy, you're making a big deal out of nothing with this trust stuff—"

"Big deal about *nothing*!" she echoed furiously. Suddenly it seemed as if they were arguing in two different dimensions, talking on two different planes. Maybe they always had been.

Cindy jumped out of bed and fumbled for the clothes she had shed so rapturously earlier in the evening. She retrieved her dress and stumbled over her high-heeled sandals— Oh damn, where was her underwear?

"What the hell are you doing?"

"Going home."

"Look, I'm sorry," Luke said. The words were conciliatory, but the tone was angry. "I had no idea you'd be so opposed to our living together, or that my marriage proposal would strike you as some sort of insult. We can, as you suggested, just go on as we have been."

Abandoning the search for her underwear she slid the dress over her head, heedless of her nakedness beneath it. She yanked up the zipper. "No, I don't think we can go on as we have been. In fact, I know we can't."

She jammed her feet into the sandals, grabbed her jacket as she dashed through the living room and slammed the door behind her.

LUKE'S FIRST INSTINCT was to chase after her, do anything to keep her from leaving. He was out of bed, fumbling for his clothes, when he heard her pickup start. A moment later a squeal of tires followed as it shot out of the newly concreted driveway.

He dropped the clothes and lay back on the bed, his body as inflexible as a board against the new sheets, and rigidly smothered that drag-her-back instinct.

So she had gone. Walked out. It had happened before, although not so dramatically. But Valerie hadn't been the woman Cindy was, and she had never meant to him what Cindy did....

He threw back the covers and was half out of bed again, still ready to go after her, but again he stopped short. What the hell could he say when he caught up to her? He'd already offered marriage. She'd rejected not only that but every other kind of relationship between them.

Okay, so his timing might have been off, he reluctantly admitted to himself. Maybe he should have waited until he really wanted the full commitment of marriage before saying anything, instead of making what had obviously sounded to her like a half-hearted offer. But he wanted to share his daily life with her now, even if he was still wrestling with misgivings that lingered from the past. He wanted her smile in the morning and her companionship in the kitchen and her wild, sweet lovemaking in the bedroom. He wanted her love....

Yet if she loved him, as she said she did, why had she walked out? Maybe she was simply as untrustworthy as Valerie had been, ready to disappear when things got rough or didn't go her way. He hadn't proposed exactly what she'd wanted, so zoom—she was gone.

Maybe he was better off without her. Work had filled his life before; it could again.

Yet that thought was little comfort as the bed stretched out big and empty around him...and the emptiness between the sheets was nothing compared to the hollow in his heart.

11

CINDY LOOKED AT THE PHONE, waiting for it to ring. She listened for the sound of a car pulling into her driveway.

Neither sound materialized. No ring of the phone, no roar of an engine. Only the empty thunder of her heartbeat and the lonely brush of a branch against the kitchen window.

She took a deep, steadying breath, willing herself not to panic. People had quarrels. They made up. This wasn't necessarily the end.

But deep down inside she knew this was more than a simple quarrel between them. This went so deep that her body felt cold beneath the satin and velvet clinging to her bare skin.

The next few days of silence emphasized that unhappy fact. Sometimes she berated herself for walking out. He had, albeit a bit grudgingly, offered to go on as they had been. Perhaps she should have settled for that. But she honestly couldn't conceive of any intimate relationship—marriage, living together or just maintaining the status quo—surviving without trust. And the way he had brushed off the importance of trust both hurt and infuriated her.

Okay, fine, she told herself defiantly as the time with no word from Luke lengthened. It was probably for the best that he hadn't come after her. Because if he had, she would likely have fallen into his arms and whisked this problem of trust under the carpet...where it would have hidden until it burst out and destroyed their relationship eventually, anyway.

She briefly considered trying somehow to prove her rock-solid trustworthiness to him. She had little fantasies of risking her life to save his. Rushing in to save him from his burning apartment. Faithfully nursing him back to health from some life-threatening illness. But no such dramatic opportunities arose; he neither set his apartment afire nor caught some debilitating disease, and she could almost have laughed at herself and the foolish little fantasies . . . if she weren't so near tears.

A couple of times she tried to call him, but she put the phone down without speaking when his answering machine came on, uncertain of what she had intended to say. Several times she drove by his apartment, but his car was never there. The local newspaper did a big article on Winds Unlimited, and Luke was quoted several times. He sounded important and busy. Apparently he had easily slipped back into his old ways, and work, not her, was all he needed. There was no reason for them to talk.

But she loved him regardless, and what was she going to do about that?

She abandoned the implausible little fantasies and faced the pain of her loss. Someday the ache inside her would fade. Someday she'd be able to whisper his name without feeling a dry constriction in her throat. She had survived the lost love of gymnastics and eventually found in it the comfort of an old friend.

She'd do that with her love for Luke, too. Accept her loss and survive and go on with life. Someday she'd get over loving Luke.

Yes. And someday the winds would stop blowing and the tides stop rising and falling. . .

LUKE CHOSE the obvious solution to fill the hole in his life: work. A company accountant was hospitalized, and he temporarily took over that job as well as his own. He spent most of his time in Portland. He pored over figures at night, looking for ways to cut costs. He worked up a new approach to the meetings with investors.

His enthusiasm for the project increased, as did his enthusiasm for the value of making practical use of wind energy in general. There were problems in getting the costs down to compete effectively with other sources of energy, but that was a challenge for the young industry, not an insurmountable barrier.

Yes, work was all he needed, he told himself for at least the hundredth time. On a rare night at the apartment, he was shuffling through the pages spread across his dining-room table. Work was definitely more dependable than some volatile relationship in which a man was never quite certain where he stood. Cindy had made it plain enough that she wanted nothing more to do with him. He loved her. He'd offered to marry her—and still she'd walked out.

His back hurt from sitting too long in one position. He stood up, stretched and arched his spine and tried not to remember the magic of Cindy's hands massaging his taut muscles. He walked across the living room and looked out at the rocky stretch of beach that was visible by moonlight.

Suddenly he yanked the drapes shut. Sometimes he wished he'd never taken this apartment with its damned ocean view. Looking at the beach always reminded him of Cindy. Sometimes when he saw a figure walking there he'd even think for a moment that it was her. But it never was.

He turned and looked at the open door to the darkened bedroom. And he damned sure wished he'd never bought that king-size bed. Every night that he slept in it reminded him of how big and empty it was without her. Maybe he ought to move up to Portland where there wouldn't be so many reminders.

He stalked back to the papers on the table, impatient and angry with himself for letting his thoughts turn, again, to her.

WEEKDAY BUSINESS at the kite shop had finally slowed after a spell of unusually warm, mild fall weather had ended, but weekends were still busy. The main store up in Astoria called to say it was sending down an experimental model of a kite design that Cindy had sent them earlier, the first box kite she'd designed. They thought there might be some problems with it. Joanna's pregnancy was now a pronounced tummy bulge, of which she was smugly proud. Cindy had grown closer to Melanie, whose husband's truck-driving job sometimes took him away from home for two or three weeks at a time.

Cindy was pleased and proud of her students. They were a long way from being ready for competitive events, but she thought it was time to put on an exhibition to let the parents see their children's progress. She talked it over with the kids, and together they chose a Thursday night. She sent slips home with them to invite parents and friends to come. And as the night approached, she knew she was as excited about it as the children were.

THE COMPANY, OF COURSE, was more than willing to let Luke work his tail off; they gladly kept throwing more and more work his way. He now had the company's financial matters organized to the point where he could, if he chose, take most weekends and evenings off. So far, still trying to make work fill his life, he hadn't chosen to do that. He loved the job, found it more challenging and satisfying than any work he'd ever done, but he had also gradually become aware that it was a bottomless hole that would cheerfully swallow every bit of time and energy he'd let it have—and still not fill *him* up. He missed Cindy even when he was at his busiest.

Several times there were blank spaces on his answering machine where someone had called but hadn't left a message after the beep. If the caller was Cindy, he realized ruefully, she was probably more certain than ever that he was an incurable workaholic.

Would it make any difference to her if he could convince her he wasn't?

He'd have to do more than simply tell her so, of course. His excitement grew at the idea of figuring out a concrete way to patch things up between them. He'd have to prove it to her with his actions. And the first step was not to *be* a single-minded workaholic. For starters, he resolutely limited the company's monopolization of his time.

He knew which evenings she was at the health club conducting classes. He went by the club and arranged for a trial membership. On a Thursday evening he went to use the pool for the first time. He decided that after the gymnastics class would be the best time to run into Cindy "accidentally."

He swam and worked out on a couple of machines, keeping a close eye on the time, not wanting to miss Cindy after the class was over. He showered and dressed. When he went out to the reception area, he heard applause from the room where Cindy's classes were held.

"What's going on?" he asked an attendant.

"The gymnastics students are giving an exhibition tonight."

Luke slipped into the room, sorry that he hadn't known earlier. He would have liked to have watched the whole program. Apparently it was almost over now. The children lined up and took turns running at a minitrampoline. Each child would bounce once, and then, with varying degrees of proficiency, do a number of different jumps onto a big, soft mat. Cindy announced that Tracy would then give the final performance of the evening. She was obviously the class's star pupil. She raced through a series of twists and flips like an energetic little elf in a pink leotard, and there was no doubt in Luke's mind that Cindy was a terrific coach. He, along with the others in the audience, applauded enthusiastically.

Cindy brought all the students, including several small boys, back for a bow. Luke applauded again, but he had eyes only for Cindy.

She was wearing a black leotard, feet in flexible little gymnastics slippers like those the children wore, pale hair in the elegant coil she wore only for gymnastics. She looked slim and lovely and a little ethereal, every inch the woman of mystery who had haunted his thoughts after that first encounter in the moonlight months before. And at the same time she was temptingly sexy and desirable . . . and protectively maternal, as well, as the children clustered around her.

He swallowed hard. He loved her. He needed her . . . but she looked as if she was doing just fine without him. But he would convince her he'd changed if he had to wrap her up in one of those mats and make her listen to him. He wasn't married to his work, and he wanted her to know that. He wanted to be married to *her*.

It took a while for the room to clear. People stood around talking and visiting. Luke fidgeted. He wished he had some giant broom and could just sweep everyone out the door. He left the room, thinking he'd wait in his car, then hurried back, afraid he'd miss her. He figured he had to catch her in some semipublic place, because she might simply refuse to talk to him if he went to the cottage or telephoned her.

Finally the last mutual congratulations between parents and teacher were spoken, the last child complimented and encouraged, and everyone was gone. Luke stepped out from behind the tier of seats where he'd been lurking.

"Hi," he said, as if this were some casual meeting rather than an encounter he'd planned with the deliberation of a stock market move.

She jumped slightly at the sound of an unexpected voice, but her expression didn't give away anything when she saw him. "Hello." After a moment's wary hesitation she added, "You came to the exhibition?"

"Actually, no. Although I would have if I'd known about it."

She folded her arms in a you-expect-me-to-believe-that attitude. It was not an auspicious beginning, and he searched for something with a neutral content to continue the conversation.

"I see you have more mats now. And equipment."

A vaulting horse stood in one corner. Guy wires anchored a set of uneven parallel bars in place at the far end of the room. There was also a balance beam with metal legs, plus another beam without legs lying flat on the floor. He remembered Cindy's saying the students had to start out that way and gradually work up to the beam's full four-foot height.

"The health club bought the equipment. We've worked out a different arrangement, and I'm actually a part-time member of the staff now. That relieves me of business and financial matters, so I can concentrate on coaching. We were fortunate enough to pick up equipment very cheaply from a Portland gymnastics academy that was going out of business."

"I see you also have some boys in class now."

"Yes. I can teach them the basics, although we don't yet have the equipment for the men's events, so I can take them only so far. I also feel better qualified to teach women's events, of course."

"Tracy looked terrific. You're doing a great job with her. And with the other students, as well, I'm sure."

"Thank you." Her tone was polite but considerably less appreciative than the words. She didn't seem inclined to continue the conversation.

"You have more students than you did earlier."

"Taking my class has apparently become something of an 'in' thing for the local children to do." She sounded uncertain whether to be amused or chagrined by that. He supposed it meant she got some pint-sized klutzes in her class, perhaps planted there by competitive mothers. Then she asked bluntly, "If you didn't come to see the exhibition, why are you here?"

Because I love you, sweet Cinnamon. Because I can't live without you. But he had to prove something else to her first.

"I signed up for a trial membership with the health club. I have more free time now, and the swimming is fun and relaxing. Everyone needs to make time for fun." He winced after the words were out. They sounded as if he was deliberately parroting something she'd once said, perhaps even mocking her. But, damn it, they were true, and he meant them.

"Winds Unlimited go broke?" she inquired.

The pleasantly spoken question made him blink. "Of course not. The company is doing great. Construction has already started. What made you ask that?"

"I couldn't think of any other reason that you'd have free time for swimming. Although I suppose you need the exercise now that you're no longer working at the mill."

"Yes, I do need the exercise," he agreed lamely. This conversation was not exactly going as he'd planned. "But I also came because I wanted to prove to you that I've changed."

For a moment something that might have been interest flickered in her eyes. "In what way?"

"Well, I'm usually free on weekends and evenings now—"

"How nice for you. Perhaps you'll have time to think about a certain discussion we had the night we were celebrating your new apartment . . . although I doubt it." She smiled, not encouragingly. "Would you excuse me, please? I have some things to do." He started to follow when she turned and walked away, but she disappeared behind a door labeled Women, effectively ending any further conversation.

Luke went back to his apartment and stood looking out the window, hands jammed in his jacket pockets. Fog blotted out the night view, and he saw only his own reflection in the glass. It was not much company.

He turned and looked across the room at the opposite wall. The diamond-shaped kite with its bright yellow color and arched rainbow looked incongruously cheerful, hardly suiting his dark mood.

Nothing he'd said or done had impressed her. Not his presence at the health club nor his claim about swimming for fun. She still thought he was the same old workaholic, and she was having no part of that.

Was there anything that would prove to her that he really had changed?

Maybe one thing.

He looked at the kite again. He had moved it from the wall of his old apartment to this one, but he had never flown it in the sky. Its cheerfulness challenged him now, and the rainbow mocked him, just as Cindy's smile had done. He gave a small, inward groan as the realization of what he had to do struck him.

Did he have to do *that*? Did he really have to do what she'd alternately teased or chided him about in order to show he'd changed? It was no big thing, and yet it was a line he'd always resisted crossing.

LUKE LOCKED HIS CAR and walked through the park to the town beach. It was a sunny Saturday afternoon, and there were both children and grown-ups around. Some were looking for rocks or driftwood; others were just walking. Fall storms had brought in more driftwood and scattered it along the beach. A couple of small boys were trying to fly a big serpent kite but not having much luck, in spite of the brisk wind. His own kite jumped and danced in his hands as if eager to get wind-borne.

He felt foolish. A grown man out here flying a kite like some carefree kid. Next he'd be chewing bubble gum or watching cartoons. And there wasn't much point in being here, anyway, he realized in frustration, because Cindy wasn't here flying kites, after all. He should have called in anonymously to the kite shop to make certain she was having a demonstration that afternoon.

Impatiently he brushed at his wind-tossed hair. Then, shrugging, he turned and started back to the car. No point in this. He'd just have to pick another day and hope for better luck next time. He was beginning to think this was a damn fool idea. Even if she'd been here, his coming to the beach and flying a kite probably wouldn't have made her change her mind. Piece by piece he'd taken apart that fiasco of a celebration at his apartment, and it was finally beginning to dawn on him that the issue of trust was more important to Cindy than his work habits. Her tart comment about his putting her on probation kept rattling around in his thoughts, although he'd brushed it off at the time. It had an uncomfortable ring of familiarity.

There was also something he wanted to tell her, even if she didn't want anything to do with him, an important bit of news he'd received. He wanted her to know the truth on that particular score, just in case she'd ever had any doubts.

She wasn't here, however, and he was undecided about what to do with the afternoon. He could go back to the apartment and study the impact of some proposed tax law changes on the wind energy industry, of course. He could do his laundry.

But what the hell, he was here; he might as well fly the damned kite for once.

That proved somewhat more difficult than he'd anticipated. Cindy always made kite flying look easy. Getting the kite in the air was no problem. He just gave it a toss into the wind, and away it went. The trick was to keep the gusty wind from making it nose-dive just as quickly back to the sand. Once it came down on a driftwood stump, and he figured he'd wrecked it for sure, but he managed to untangle it before any damage was done. He finally realized he wasn't feeding out line at the right speed, giving the kite either too much or not enough. A light tension had to be maintained.

There, it was up and flying! The feeling of success and elation surprised Luke as the kite finally soared and hovered at a respectable height. It felt like something alive up there, jerking and dancing against the taut line. Its buoyancy made him feel buoyant, too. There was something so lighthearted and exuberant about the yellow kite hanging up there in the sky, and some of its cheerfulness transmitted itself to him through the almost invisible line he held. He wished he had one of those stunt kites so he could make it swoop and climb.

The boys on the beach still hadn't gotten their kite to fly, he noticed. Every time they got it up a little way, it flopped like a fish caught on a line, and its tail dragged along the ground. They were watching his success enviously. Now that he was closer, Luke recognized them as Melanie's kids, Todd and Bobby. He hadn't seen them for some time.

"Built any more good forts lately?" he called.

"Nah. Mom says we can't play in the driftwood if an adult isn't with us. Too dangerous," Todd said. "And she's always too busy to bring us, and Dad's always gone driving truck."

"She's probably right about playing in the driftwood. Sometimes a wave sneaks in and really flings that stuff around. But flying a kite is fun, too."

"Yeah, 'cept we can't make ours fly." Bobby, the younger boy, sounded thoroughly disgruntled. The kite jerked around on the ground, its long tail flapping erratically in the wind.

"Why don't you come over here and fly my kite, and I'll see what I can do with yours?"

Luke handed the spool and line to the younger boy and went to look at the serpent that refused to fly. The boy immediately took off at gleeful run, dragging the yellow kite behind him like a wind-borne pet.

"This looks like one of those serpent kites from the Challenge the Wind store," Luke commented.

"Yeah. The lady that works there, Mom's friend, gave it to us. It worked real good for a while. But we were flying it at home, and it got tangled up in a tree, and then we had to put new line on it."

Glancing at Bobby's energetic style of kite flying, Luke suspected how the serpent kite had got tangled in a tree. He thought about saying something, but what the heck. The kid was obviously having a great good time. Maybe he should have tried running with the kite himself. It looked like fun. Luke turned his attention back to the serpent.

"I think the problem may be in the way the new line is attached to the kite. See these two places on the serpent's head? There's supposed to be a short line attached to each one. Those short lines are called the bridle. It helps keep the kite at the proper angle against the wind." Luke was rather amused with himself. Apparently he had picked up a little kite expertise from Cindy without ever realizing it. "Those two lines are supposed to join here, and that's where the main line is attached. That's called the towing point."

"Oh, yeah, I see what we did!" Todd said. He was squatting down beside Luke, man to man. "We don't have any bridle. We just fastened the main line to one of those bridle places."

Together they changed the rigging on the kite. It was more complicated getting the big serpent to fly than it had been with the small diamond. When they tossed the serpent in the air, the line kept tangling in the long, flexible tail. Finally Luke had Todd hold the serpent in the air some distance away from where Luke stood with the spool, and up it went like the flying monster it was supposed to be.

Luke cheered, and so did the boys. They took turns flying the kites. The colorful serpent, its grinning face and long tail snapping and flapping in the wind, was fun. It wasn't a stunt kite, but Luke found by trial and error that he could make it swoop a little, as if it were trying to attack something on the ground.

Finally Todd asked what time it was and then said they'd better be getting home. He reeled in the flapping serpent.

"We got another broken kite at home," Todd said. He spoke in an offhand manner, but his sideways look was hopeful.

Luke hesitated. He knew what Todd was hinting at. Their mother obviously wasn't a kite flyer or a fort builder, and their dad was temporarily too involved in making a living to give them as much time and attention as he'd no doubt like to.

He started to shake his head. He didn't want to get involved in flying kites with a couple of kids...or did he? And, on second thought, why not? Flying the kites was fun, and it was even more fun with a couple of boys to share the enjoyment. It was actually the most fun he'd had in weeks, he had to admit, thinking back over the bleak days since he and Cindy had parted. It had been at least a couple of hours since he'd had a single thought about wind turbine costs, presentations to investors or profit projections. Maybe he and the boys would just march into the kite shop and buy one of those stunt kites! He didn't know now why he'd so stubbornly resisted Cindy's many invitations to go flying with her.

"Why don't you two bring your broken kite here to the beach next weekend, and we'll see what we can do to fix it?"

Todd and Bobby both responded. "Sure!"

"Okay. Same time next Saturday. *If* it's okay with your mom. You be sure to check with her, okay? Tell her who you'll be with. I think she'll remember me. She can call me, if she'd like."

"Okay, Luke. See you next week!"

Luke was reeling in the rainbow kite when he realized they hadn't been the only kite flyers on the beach. He'd been so involved with the boys that he hadn't even noticed Cindy arrive. She had a kite he hadn't seen before. At least he guessed it was a kite; from this distance it looked like a miniature castle sitting on the ground. She didn't have it in the air yet, but the unusual structure had already drawn a small crowd of interested onlookers. The wind had suddenly grown stronger.

"WHAT IS THAT THING?"

The question came from a little girl among the onlookers, some of whom had come because of Cindy's posted notice in the kite shop announcing a test flight of a new kite design. Some of the audience had just wandered over out of curiosity.

"It's a kite, and I'm hoping to make it fly," she answered the little girl.

"It looks like a castle!"

Cindy laughed. "Haven't you ever heard of castles in the air?"

The idea for a kite that looked like a miniature castle had come to Cindy before the sand-sculpture contest, but not in time to be ready for the festival. She hoped it didn't turn out to be as impractical as "castles in the air" sounded. If it did work, they'd have several made up to sell at the festival next year.

Actually, from the way the thing seemed to want to take off, she doubted she'd have any trouble getting it to fly. In fact, as an extra-strong gust of wind hit it, she had trouble holding it down. The problem was going to be controlling the kite after it was in the air. The three-dimensional castle was basically an elaboration on a compound box kite, and big kites of that type could develop tremendous lift. Her design of this one, unfortunately, also seemed to be a little off balance.

Cindy got everything ready and then glanced down the beach one more time before sending the big castle kite aloft.

She had seen a man and two boys flying a couple of kites down there. The man was reeling his kite in now. He looked remarkably like Luke. Same tall, lean build; same dark hair; same athletic way of moving.

But it couldn't be Luke, of course. He wouldn't waste a Saturday afternoon flying kites with two little boys. This was just some doting father who happened to look a little like Luke, out with his sons for an afternoon.

Cindy turned back to her own kite. She had only to release it to send it surging upward. The wind had strengthened perceptibly in just the past few minutes. Perhaps she should have waited until the wind wasn't so strong to—

Then she had no time to think about what she should have done. The kite took off as if some demented king was in control of the castle. Instead of rising smoothly upward, it angled across the beach, and it had so much pull that it dragged Cindy right with it.

She dodged a driftwood stump lying on its side, tried to anchor the line to a tentacled root and missed. Off she went again, dragged along like some tin can bouncing behind a honeymooner's car. If she could just get her balance for a moment—

The overbalanced kite turned a peculiar half somersault, momentarily offering a little slack on the line, and Cindy grabbed the chance to dig her heels into the sand and catch her breath. Her audience had been left behind.

"Hey, you okay?"

Luke! He ran up to her and grabbed the reel holding the kite line, easing some of the strain on her arms.

Her hair was in her mouth, her arms felt as if they'd nearly been pulled out of their sockets, and she was out of breath. But she managed to gasp, "I'm fine! Of course I'm fine." She hadn't been "fine" in weeks and wasn't now, but she wasn't about to admit that to Luke. "I'm just trying out this new kite."

"Looks to me as if it may be trying *you* out."

"The design may need a few—" the kite leaped like an untamed bronc on the end of a lariat, jerking them both forward "—few adjustments."

"Can I do anything to help?"

"You don't know anything about kite flying."

"Sure I do." He moved behind her so that he could reach around her and hang on to the reel with both hands. He braced his feet and used his weight against the pull of the big kite, making them both lean backward. "I've spent the past couple of hours flying that kite you gave me. And helping Melanie's boys fly the serpent you gave them."

So it had been Luke she'd seen with the boys! "I'm impressed," she admitted. "I never thought you'd do it."

"I guess I wanted you to see that I could have fun flying a kite. And it really was fun. I finally got it through my head that kites aren't just for the young. They're for the young at heart."

She looked as if she might want to believe he meant that but wasn't totally convinced. "Where's your kite now?"

"I dropped it and ran to catch up with you when I saw you were in trouble. Look, could we go somewhere and talk? This shouting back and forth on the end of a kite line isn't the greatest form of communication."

"I can't. I'm working. I'm test-flying this kite. I designed it." As if to challenge her, it gave a lurch at the end of the line. It wasn't flying upright as it was supposed to, but kept tilting over on one side. Cindy jerked the line, but the big kite and heavy wind combined to treat her puny attempt at control with scorn.

"Okay, then, you'll just have to listen to what I have to say right here. Just in case you ever had any doubts about my innocence, I got a letter from my lawyer. He says the real embezzler has been caught. Apparently the company thought I was guilty—but they were watching other employees just in case I wasn't. So when he got greedy and thought he could get away with it just once more, they nailed him."

"I'm glad—but I never doubted you! I told you that! That was never the problem."

Cindy's audience had begun to catch up with them. She felt foolish, standing there with Luke's arms around her, shouting personal information back and forth. But apparently it didn't bother him, judging by the next words he shouted at her.

"What did you say?" she asked, certain she must have misunderstood him.

"I said, will you marry me? I love you. I know you turned me down once, and maybe I shouldn't be asking again so soon, but—"

The kite took off down the beach, as if it had deigned to let them hold it in one place long enough. Not even Luke's weight added to Cindy's could stop it. Cindy stumbled and fell, dragging Luke down with her. That slowed but didn't stop the kite. They tumbled along the beach behind it, leaving a series of ruts in the sand.

"Let's let it go!" Luke yelled.

"No!"

"You haven't changed a bit. You're as stubborn as ever!"

Cindy hadn't time to argue the point. They were heading toward the thick jumble of driftwood at the far end of the beach. She thought she might be able to get the line wrapped around something heavy enough to stop the kite there. Luke got to his feet for a moment, but then they both went sprawling again.

"I know kite flying can be great, but I'm kind of new at this. Are we having fun now?"

Cindy's foot scraped across a rock, her tired shoulders ached, and she felt as if she had enough sand in her hair to start her own beach. "We're having a terrific time!" she vowed fiercely.

Somehow, in spite of being dragged and tumbled across the sand, Luke managed to plant a kiss on her cheek, and she got a glimpse of his smile. "Yeah, we are, aren't we?"

When the kite pulled them into the jumbled driftwood, Luke snagged the line on a branch projecting from a driftwood log. He wrapped the line around the branch several times, then jammed the reel under his body to hold it secure. Cindy was under there, too. The anchored castle bounced and danced in the sky above them, and the silvered driftwood surrounded them like some fantasy forest.

"Okay, the kite isn't going to drag us off. Now you have to talk to me. Will you marry me?"

"You're so busy with work that . . . that you probably wouldn't have time for the ceremony, much less a honeymoon."

"I just promised those two boys that I'd meet them next week and fix a kite for them. If I have time for that, I think I can find time for a wedding and honeymoon. Cindy, I have changed, honestly. I've learned how to keep work and play . . . and love . . . in perspective."

"Maybe you have learned that—but I'm not sure you know what love is really all about."

He brushed a sandy streak from her cheek. "Then suppose you tell me."

"Luke, I love you. You say you love me, too, but you don't trust me, and I don't see how we could make living together or marriage or anything work when you don't trust me."

"Which is what you kept trying to tell me that night."

"You suggested we live together, and I was ready to accept until I realized that it meant entirely different things to each of us. To you it was a . . . a kind of test."

"I was putting you on probation."

"Yes! And under the circumstances, marriage would have been just a different type of probation, with me still trying to prove to you that I was trustworthy."

"So you turned down everything and walked out."

"Luke, when I said we couldn't go on as we had been, did you take it to mean that I never wanted to see you again?"

"Yes, I guess I did."

"What I meant was that we couldn't go on as we had been, with you distrusting me. But I don't suppose you can understand that, can you?"

"I couldn't at the time," he admitted. "But with a little forceful encouragement from you, I think it has finally got through to me. I was doing the same thing to you that the company did to me. I couldn't live with that, and you couldn't either. You walked out on me for much the same reasons that I walked out on the company. I don't know why it's been so difficult for me to get that through my head. But it has been."

"Luke, I've never even been certain what you thought I might do! I had these crazy little fantasies about proving myself to you. I kept wishing some big crisis would come along so that I could show you how dependable and trustworthy I was. But you didn't get yourself stranded on a rock on the incoming tide, so that I could risk my life by swimming out to rescue you. You didn't get yourself trapped in a burning building so I could dash in and save you."

He smiled. "Pretty inconsiderate of me, wasn't it?"

"You're just so . . . so damned self-sufficient that you don't need anyone."

"Yes, I do. I need you. You could marry me and save me from a wasted life of terrible loneliness and pointless wandering." When she didn't answer his affectionate teasing, he shook his head ruefully, sending a little shower of sand around them. "It was pretty damned egotistical of me to imply that you were trying to pressure me into marriage, wasn't it? Especially when it wasn't true. I'm not the greatest catch in the world."

"You might be," Cindy said softly, "if you could just trust me. Luke, what is it you don't trust? What is the awful thing you think I might do?"

"Surely you know. After the way everyone deserted and turned against me—"

"I'm not one of your business colleagues!" she protested fiercely. "I love you! Isn't my love enough to prove I'm worthy of your trust? How can you lump me in with them?"

He hesitated. The wind rattled a loose bit of driftwood overhead, but here in the shelter of logs and stumps there was a small pocket of calm.

"Once... someone else said she loved me, too. But when the chips were down, she backed off just like all the others."

"The woman you were engaged to?" Cindy was shocked. It hadn't occurred to her that this person, too, might have deserted him. She'd assumed they had drifted apart before the crisis.

"Yes. Valerie. She also worked for the Marianna Funds. She said it would be better if we 'cooled' our relationship until things blew over. I suppose she figured she had to look out for herself. I don't know. I just know she wasn't there when I needed her."

"And you thought I might do the same thing."

Softly, as if he regretted having to say the words, he pointed out, "You did it that night. You walked out. So it was an... understandable suspicion, wouldn't you say?"

Yes, reluctantly she had to admit it was. Now she had a much better understanding of why trust came so hard for him. She'd faced failure and come to terms with it, but it had been her own failure. She'd never had others fail her. His experience made her feel helpless, as if she were fighting some invisible but invincible enemy, and her weapons had no substance. The only real weapon she had was herself and what she was.

"Luke, did I disappear when you told me some people thought you were an embezzler?"

"No. As I recall, you just did strange things to my ear."

"Did I disappear when you didn't get the job with the stock brokerage company in Portland?"

"No, you were right there. Giving me hell about my attitude again."

"But I was there. And I'll always be there, if you want me." When he didn't reply, her chest rose in a long, discouraged sigh. "But just saying it isn't enough, is it? Recognizing our problem doesn't necessarily solve it. Apparently, unless some crisis comes along where I can prove myself, we have an unsolvable problem."

"I think we may be in the midst of that very crisis right now."

She felt his body stiffen over hers, and she suddenly realized they weren't exactly alone in the jumbled driftwood. Various members of her audience had finally caught up with them and were now peering over the logs and around the stumps. Since the castle kite was flying overhead to mark the spot, Cindy and Luke's whereabouts were not exactly top secret. At the moment, however, no one was looking at the kite. They seemed considerably more interested in the sight of Cindy and Luke all wound up in kite string, sand, driftwood and each other.

"What kind of crisis?"

"Everyone okay here?" one of the men asked suspiciously.

"Unless you care to stand up and assure these people that this isn't exactly what it looks like, that I'm not holding you down and ravishing you—"

Cindy scrambled out from beneath him. "Everything is fine!" she assured the onlookers. "I was just demonstrating to my. . . my fiancé here how *not* to fly a kite." In a low voice she added to Luke, "Does my saving you from potential mob violence prove anything?"

"It's good enough for me. Does your calling me a fiancé prove anything? Maybe that you'll marry me?"

"Yes—providing you'll help me get this monstrosity of a kite back to the pickup somehow."

Luke looked up at the tipsy castle bouncing overhead. At the moment, the thing looked as if it might easily carry them into the next county. Of course, if he was going there with Cindy, he didn't really mind.

"It's a deal. I love you, you know, Cindy. And love and trust go together. They really do."

Sweet Cinnamon, the spice of his life. He watched her cautiously untie the kite, then reached out and got a firm grip on her. He knew he could also be confident that life with her was never going to be dull.

Harlequin Temptation

COMING NEXT MONTH

#161 TOMORROW'S LOVE SONG Georgia Bockoven

The letter from her father arrived twenty-five years late, but when it did, Amy's fate was sealed. She was forced to use Mark Sterling to right a terrible wrong, and to risk losing him forever....

#162 TRADE SECRETS Carla Neggers

Juniper Killibrew was as prickly as her namesake plant. She prided herself on that—that and her dedication to the family firm. But when Cal Gilliam slipped the firm out from under her, he showed her how soft she really was....

#163 FIRST MATES Joanna Gilpin

When Julie Thorne decided to take a quick trip down memory lane, she didn't expect to find a fishing boat tied to her old dock. Nor did she expect to take a sensuous detour with rugged Captain Dan McLeod.

#164 CARDINAL RULES Barbara Delinsky

At first, Corinne was wary of the infamous "cardinal," Corey Haraden. She had no desire to become just one of the flock. But bombarded by his charm, she threw caution to the winds and tried her wings....